Wisdom & Folly: Sisters

Part One

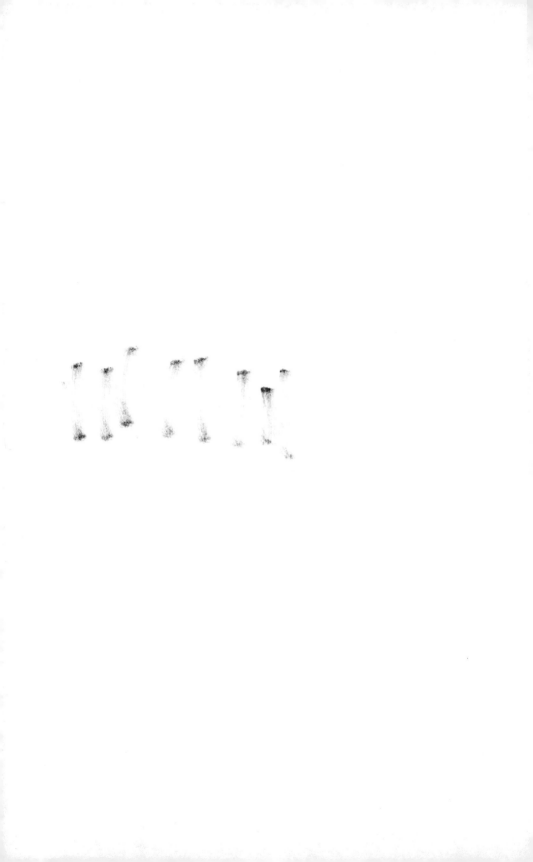

Wisdom & Folly: Sisters

Part One

Michele Israel Harper

Love2ReadLove2Write Publishing, LLC
Indianapolis, Indiana

© 2015 Michele Israel Harper

Published by Love2ReadLove2Write Publishing, LLC
Indianapolis, Indiana
www.love2readlove2writepublishing.com

Library of Congress Cataloging-in-Publication Data is on file at the Library of Congress, Washington, DC.

ISBN: 1943788006
ISBN-13: 978-1-943788-00-2
Library of Congress Control Number: 2015916503

Cover Design by Sara Helwe (www.sara-helwe.com)
"Wisdom" Model—Georgia Stanwix, Photography by Cathleen Tarawhiti
"Folly" Model—Ruxandra (www.methyss-design.com), Photography by Claudiu Miron
Wings by Katie Litchfield

To my darling Ben,
Blaze and Maverick,
Gwenivere.

I love you.

Chapter One

Then I (Wisdom) was beside Him as a master craftsman; and I was daily His delight, rejoicing always before Him, rejoicing in His inhabited world, and my delight was with the sons of men.
Proverbs 8:30-31

"Oh, Lord, it's lovely."

"Yes, it is."

His heavy hands rested lightly on her shoulders. She leaned into His touch.

"Each design is flawless," she continued.

"And perfectly executed by My master craftsman."

A thrill coursed through Wisdom at her Maker's praise. She removed her scrutiny from the brightly colored orb spinning at her feet and turned to meet His eyes. Their warm depths drew her in and set her heart ablaze.

"Oh!" Wisdom spun back around. "I've checked and rechecked, and each planet is seamlessly in orbit to support life on terra. There is a perfect balance of water and atmospheric pressure. Oh, yes! The dry land seems to be holding the waters in their place quite nicely. Also—"

"Wisdom."

She stopped her calculations and glanced over her shoulder. "Yes?"

He was laughing at her; his always smiling eyes smiling even further.

"I know. I designed it. You can rest easy now, love. It is good."

She nodded. A quick glance to the earth told her He was right. She just wanted to be *certain*. He had, after all, given her the task to carry out His most fun project to date. Movement on the globe snagged her attention. She did not realize a lengthy silence had passed until her Master chuckled.

"What do you think of the man and woman I put in My paradise?"

"They are delightful, my Lord. I can't get over how much they look like You!"

She sighed and rested her elbows on the glass blueprints spread out before her, floating mid-air. The map supported her, not shifting under her slight weight.

"Look at how much fun they're having!" she laughed.

Her eyes easily picked out the two newest creatures frolicking in the Creator's garden, far below her.

"Sheer delight," she murmured, unable to take her eyes from them.

Wisdom laughed as the woman splashed water on Adam from a pool when he wasn't looking. Adam caught her around the waist and tickled her, bending his head for a passionate kiss.

"Guard it well, for its loveliness cannot last forever."

Wisdom glanced quickly at her Lord. Seriousness had overtaken His lighthearted attitude of seconds before.

"Yes, my Love."

She bowed her head, but a slight frown creased her forehead as her mind raced. What did He mean its loveliness would not last forever? It was perfect. What could have changed His demeanor so?

"Do you think I should...?" she began.

"Oh gracious and mighty majesty!"

Whispers traveled the room as Lucifer strutted into the King's antechamber. A smile turned up the corners of Wisdom's lips. Excellent. A visit from Lucifer would brighten the King's countenance. Other angels may tease her of being the Lord's favorite, but, if He had a favorite, she was certain it would be Lucifer.

Genuine pleasure lit the King's face.

"Ah, Lucifer, My beloved, have you seen My earth?"

"I have, my lord."

She watched Lucifer preen and bow deeply as the angels in the room followed his every movement, their eyes riveted on him. His forehead very nearly touching the crystal floor, Lucifer held the bow for an inordinate amount of time, his iridescent wings splayed far on either side of him.

Wisdom's hungry eyes drank in—and were always satisfied by—the beauty her Lord created. Lucifer's exquisiteness rivaled any of the Maker's creations, including His new earth and the creatures in it.

Wisdom's gaze drifted the length of the shimmering robe pooled far behind the kneeling cherub.

Colors wafted and curled through the glass floor at random, but they could not compete with the glistening cloak. Vibrant threads wove in and out of the fabric, holding tight to precious stones of every variety.

Wisdom grinned in satisfaction as she thought of a few of those very stones being tucked deep within terra's crust. Love's creatures would be exhilarated when they found them!

Lucifer lifted his head, letting his gaze trail across the angels in the room. He seemed to enjoy the stares that followed him wherever he went. Wisdom smiled when his eyes halted on her. He straightened and speared her with an unreadable glance before turning his attention to the King. And his back to Wisdom.

It's as it should be. All focus on the Master, Wisdom thought to herself when his actions unsettled her. She tried to focus on Love's voice.

"And what do you think of My latest creation, Day Star?"

Lucifer made his way regally to the edge of the open palace, pausing at the side of the Creator.

"Well, it's great, don't get me wrong, but there are a few things I would change about it."

Audible gasps sucked the air out of the room, and Wisdom stared at Lucifer, aghast. No one had questioned the Almighty's handiwork before; it had always been perfect. It was perfect. What could Lucifer mean? Wisdom spun to look at her Creator.

Infinite sorrow rested in His eyes.

"And what would that be, beloved cherub?" He gently asked.

As Lucifer paced, he flung his hand in the direction of the new planet, its vibrant blues and greens reflecting off of his pristine face.

"Take water, for instance. It doesn't make sense. Those weak creatures you put there can't even live in it. Sure, it is pretty in its own way, but too much of the earth's surface is covered with it. If you loved those things so much, why would you make such a great deal of the earth uninhabitable for them?"

Wisdom stepped forward.

"Oh, but you see, water is necessary for life. The moisture in the air, a place for the animals of the sea to live—it has been perfectly calculated..."

"And that's another thing," Lucifer cut her off with a scathing look.

Pink tinged Wisdom's cheeks as she stumbled back. She had never seen such a look on an angel's face before. Gooseflesh trailed her arms, and she rubbed at it, trying to still the clenching in her gut. What had she done wrong?

"Why did you make those fabulous creatures of yours so weak? I would have placed giant beasts as masters of *my* world, not made so many things larger than, and capable of trampling, my so-called rulers."

Lucifer clasped his hands behind his back and faced the sphere, pride shining off of his entire being. Wisdom watched him hesitantly turn in the King's direction when He did not speak. Squirming, Lucifer bowed when their eyes met.

"But, of course, all you do is perfect."

"Of course."

Lucifer straightened and hurried from the room.

Tears filled Wisdom's eyes when she saw the pain on her Master's face. She opened her mouth to speak.

"Leave me, please, everyone."

All in the room bowed and hastened to obey.

Yearning to comfort Him, Wisdom cast one last glance back at her Love before the doors swung soundlessly shut.

❀ ❀ ❀

Prudence lounged on the gold-threaded settee, barely stifling a yawn. Káel, handsome though he was, was droning on and on and on about the beauty and the majesty and the glory of the lord.

Awesome as that was and all, sometimes Prudence just wanted to talk about something else.

Angels have other interests, you know, she scolded Káel silently as she tried to look interested.

The door burst open, and Prudence lazily looked its way, wondering what glorious thing the lord had done now. Likely some angel was in an uproar over the littlest thing.

She jumped to her feet.

Lucifer stood at the door, both hands braced against the doorframe. He breathed heavily and stared at the floor, his shoulders bowed under a heavy, unseen burden.

Prudence started toward him.

"Wait, Pru! Don't you want to hear what happened next?"

"Not now, Káel! Can't you see Lucifer is distressed?"

She shook off Káel's restraining hand and hurried toward Lucifer. She reached out to touch him, then jerked her hand back. He had said never to touch him without invitation. But, oh, how she wanted to run her hand over the porcelain skin of his hand. Or just briefly nudge one precious gem. Just once.

"Lucifer? Are you...? Is everything...is everything okay?"

Lucifer glanced up at her. She met his gaze boldly before dropping her head in respect.

"Prudence. Valor. Aurik. With me. Now."

Prudence hesitated, surprised, but Lucifer was already moving away. She rushed to catch up, desperate to be at his side.

Lucifer stopped in other rooms, calling only a few angels from each task.

Prudence's chest swelled as she realized she was the first angel he called. She made sure she stayed close to him as others joined them. She admired the way he strode with purpose, his mantle sweeping far behind him. Her heart hammered when he swiftly led them to his very own abode.

She stared in awe at the mansion she had never before been inside. She had dreamed of this day. Reverently stepping over the threshold, Prudence hurried after Lucifer to a chamber deep within the house. He made a great show of pulling the doors tightly closed.

Dropping his face into one hand, he braced his other hand against the wall and froze.

Prudence glanced around, then smirked. If he was trying to get their attention, he had succeeded.

"You know He can still see and hear us behind closed doors," joked one of the angels.

Lucifer ignored the comment, and the room slid into a strained silence.

"Brothers, Sisters—I have news."

His rich voice poured from behind his hand, and Prudence shivered with delight. He was such a pleasure to listen to.

"The master, the creator, he—he no longer listens to me."

He swept his hand down his face and gazed at the ceiling.

"I fear—I fear I have outgrown my usefulness."

Prudence sucked in her breath.

Never, she vowed.

Cries and objections fluctuated in volume.

He blinked hard, but his eyes remained dry. Lucifer held up his hands.

"Yes, yes, I am afraid it is true. He no longer cares for me, or for some of you, if what you have told me in the past is true. He is not doing what is in my—I mean, *our*—best interests."

A cacophony of voices exploded in disbelief and worry and fear.

Prudence's brow furrowed. Why didn't this feel right?

"That is not true."

Aurik's voice rose boldly above the rest.

Prudence bristled. What Lucifer had to say was uncomfortable, but he would never say something that wasn't true.

The room quieted. Lucifer's cold gaze met Aurik's fiery one. "What did you say?"

"I said; it's not the truth. Everything the Lord does is kind, and good, and true, and just. He cares for us."

"Oh, he cares, does he?" Lucifer called and swept his arms and wings wide. "What of the new creatures he made? The new planet, the galaxy, the universe? He is giving our reign to those...those *things*. They are not just his latest toys; they are our replacements! He is exchanging us for them. He is done with each and every one of you, just wait and see if I'm right. Now, if *I* were in charge, I would set these weak beings aside and make sure none of you ever feared replacement."

"I'm not going to listen to these...blasted...*un*truths."

Aurik pushed his way from the room, jerking the doors next to Lucifer open. Lucifer inclined his head and waited for Aurik to pass.

"Anyone else?" His frigid voice held none of the passion from moments before.

Two more angels left the room, but far less boldly. One glanced behind her as Lucifer closed and fastened the door.

Prudence made sure that angel saw her scorn before turning her full attention back to Lucifer.

"Now, where were we? Ah, yes. The king is done with us, I'm afraid."

"But, Lucifer, mighty one, what are we going to do?" cried Abundance.

"Worry not, dear friends. I have a plan. Prudence, my dear, come here. I want you by my side."

Prudence walked forward; afraid she would burst. Facing the room of angels, she lived her dearest wish. At Lucifer's side, above them all.

Chapter Two

I, Wisdom, dwell with Prudence.
Proverbs 8:12

Angels gathered in clusters, all whispering and glancing toward the throne room.

"Lucifer said *what?*"

Hurrying past, Wisdom grimaced as she caught a hint of conversation.

She scanned the other angels' faces. Their expressions were usually full of joy and laughter, and their whispers, hushed and excited. Now creases danced across faces that had never worn such lines before. And the whispers were strained and somber.

Too bad the whispers aren't full of laughter and teasing this time, Wisdom mourned.

Reaching her slender dwelling stretching far above her head, Wisdom slipped inside.

Discretion greeted her at the entryway.

"Is everything ok? I heard what happened."

Wisdom sank onto the plush, satin-covered bench by the door.

"I don't know what to think. How can Lucifer talk to Him like that? I don't understand."

Prudence burst through the front entrance, bouncing the crystalline door off the wall with a jarring *crack*.

"Can you believe it? Can you believe what happened?" Prudence demanded.

"No, I can't, and I was there," moaned Wisdom.

Discretion bustled over and closed the door Prudence had left wide open. It turned a swirling blue-gold opaque once it clicked shut.

Wisdom dropped her head into her hands.

"I can't believe it at all."

"Me neither. If the lord had just listened to Lucifer, the world would be a much better place."

Wisdom's head shot up.

"Hush, sister, you do not know of what you speak!" burst from Discretion's mouth.

"Yes, I do! Lucifer came and told us straightaway. The lord just threw out all of his suggestions, not even caring what Lucifer thought. And he, the highest and most beautiful angel in heaven!"

Wisdom looked at Prudence askance.

"That's not exactly what happened…"

Prudence continued as if Wisdom had never spoken.

"Oh, yeah, and one of the mere *craftsmen* was there and dared interrupt when he was having a private conversation with the master. The nerve of some angels!"

"That 'mere craftsman' happened to be me," Wisdom interjected dryly.

If Prudence heard, she gave no indication.

"I just wish he showed Lucifer the same courtesy he shows the rest of the heavenly beings. Lucifer deserves it." Prudence sighed. She leaned against the translucent table that was changing colors at whim, a dreamy look entering her eyes. "Lucifer is just—just, *wonderful.*"

Alarmed, Wisdom glanced at Discretion. Discretion stared back with wide eyes. Both moved as one to Prudence's side.

"Be careful, sister."

"Are you sure you are not ascribing worship to one of the Lord's created beings, instead of Himself?"

"I would be cautious of anything Lucifer says."

"Especially if it goes against the Lord."

Prudence broke away from her sisters.

"Oh for heaven's sake, you two are being ridiculous. I'm not going against what the lord says. I'm just stating an opinion. My opinion."

"How is that not going against our Maker?" Wisdom demanded.

Prudence rolled her eyes and huffed.

"Never mind. It doesn't matter. Everything will work out just fine."

Prudence turned away from them, but not before Wisdom saw excitement glistening in her eyes.

"Oh yes, Lucifer said everything would work out perfectly."

"Pru…"

Wisdom's hand felt empty as Prudence shrugged out of the feather-light touches of her sisters.

"I, uh, I'm going to my room."

Prudence unfurled her wings and brushed their feathery tips against the waterfalls on either wall as she hurried away, something she had done since Wisdom had built their dwelling and Discretion had installed the cascades on every available surface.

The site both warmed and chilled Wisdom. Normal, yet not at all. What was wrong with Prudence?

Wisdom watched her flick her wings, sprinkling water droplets on the luminous walls, floors, and ceiling before disappearing inside her room.

The door closed with a firm *thud*, and Wisdom and Discretion looked at each other, neither saying a word.

The tinkling of the many waterfalls cascading down the clear walls mingled with birdsong out the open window.

Wisdom's heart weighed against her chest like a stone.

"Maybe I should talk with her?"

"No," Discretion answered quickly. "She doesn't want to talk right now. Just let her work this out. She knows our Lord is good."

"Are you sure? I could…"

Discretion moved to her side and laid a gentle hand on Wisdom's shoulder.

"You know in your heart the best thing to do for her. Pray. Speak to her Creator. He'll comfort Prudence in ways we never could. Just give it to Him."

Wisdom pondered her sister's words, seeking guidance. Seeking truth. Looking at the situation from every angle possible to see if there was anything more she could do. Finally, she blew out her breath and smiled.

"You are right, sister, as always."

Discretion gave her an impish grin.

"I know."

"Oh! You!"

Wisdom dunked her fingertips in the light blue pool by the satin bench and flicked a few droplets at her sister. Sweet perfume escaped from each watery bead as they exploded and disappeared.

"Careful, sister. Remember what happened last time?"

"I still need Mercy to have a little chat with you 'bout that," grumbled Wisdom.

Discretion's smile beamed, a brilliant light in their sparkling home.

"She would just jump right in and join me. You know how she loves a good time."

"Yeah, yeah—I'm going up before I get drenched. Again."

Discretion cringed.

"How you can stand it up there…"

An enormous grin made Wisdom's gorgeous face lovelier still.

"Remind me to thank the Lord for your dislike of high places."

"Remind *me* to talk to Him about the reason for these blasted wings."

Wisdom laughed.

"To help you better swim, my dear. What else?"

"Go to your tower, dear sister, and leave us lowly land dwellers to ourselves."

Wisdom chuckled and blew Discretion a kiss. Discretion shook her head and bent to urge the stream flowing through the middle of their living room in another direction.

The girl loved water a little too much. Wisdom fully expected the day to come when Discretion transformed their home into a giant lake, and she would have to swim to get in the front door. Wisdom chuckled again as her wings lifted her to her chamber overlooking the King's palace and the stars beyond.

Wisdom's heart thrilled the farther she lifted away from the ground.

I will praise You, Creator, for the rest of my days for giving me the gift of flight!

You're welcome, came His laughing response.

Wisdom smiled and stretched her wing wide, gliding on the air currents.

She landed in the open doorway and stepped onto her wall-less, roofless chamber, blue and purple sky surrounding her on all sides. Maps and blueprints and tools littered the wide-open space, and Wisdom carefully stepped over them all, thankful that Discretion would never risk the flight to her room to organize the well-loved mess. Or install a waterfall.

She unrolled the schematics for the Andromeda galaxy and sat at her desk to study the intricate details, reminding herself that the Lord would take care of Prudence and Lucifer. She smiled at Discretion's threat of another water fight. She could always count on her sisters to calm and refocus her when she tried to take on too many tasks.

She frowned.

Well, only one sister this time, but Prudence would come around.

※ ※ ※

Prudence sat on her couch in her sparse apartment and seethed. Fists clenched, teeth bared, chest heaving. Just who did her sisters think she was? A weakling to be coddled and told what to do? What to think?

"Don't admire Lucifer, Prudence. It's wrong," she mimicked to herself, her face twisted in fury.

Don't tell us what you think, Prudence; listen to us.

Don't think for yourself, Prudence; you'll hurt something.

Prudence leapt off her couch and began to pace. Lucifer never told her what to do or how to think. He trusted her.

"At least Lucifer sees me as valuable. *He* would never dismiss what

I said as if it didn't matter," she growled into the silence.

The one and only gift the lord had seen fit to give her, unlike the multitude of gifts he had given her sisters, was the ability to see glimpses of the future. And even that had become unreliable lately. But one thing she could see clearly. Things needed to change.

She—and Lucifer—deserved respect.

And she—they—were going to get it.

A soft knock at the door made Prudence jump and whirl toward it. She unclenched her fists with great effort and plastered what she hoped was a pleasant smile on her face. Wisdom poked her head inside.

"Pru? You ok?"

"Fine."

Prudence hoped Wisdom wouldn't notice her clipped words or strained voice. She just wanted Wisdom to leave. Wisdom studied her for an uncomfortable moment.

"K. It's my watch in the Garden, but I wanted to see if you needed anything before I left."

Of course it is. You always get the fun assignments.

With great effort, Prudence kept her teeth from grinding.

"Nope." *Just go!*

"All right…" Wisdom drew the words out slowly. But still she stood there. "I love you, Prudence."

Something seized Prudence's throat like a claw and wouldn't let go. Her eyes burned and felt hot.

What is happening to me?

Prudence gave Wisdom an abrupt nod and turned her back. She waved in dismissal as a tear slipped down her cheek. She heard the door close softly behind her.

Prudence lifted the tear from her cheek with a shaking finger and stared at it.

It was nothing like the tears she had shed in the throne room in the heat of worship, loving and praising her master with abandon. This tear was completely foreign to her.

"What is happening to me?" she whispered.

Come talk to Me, dear one.

Her heart snatched and choked off the whispered words before they fully formed in her mind.

Oh, she was going to talk to him, all right. She and Lucifer were going to have a nice little chat with the lord. And *he* would listen to *them* this time.

Chapter Three

How you are fallen from heaven, O Lucifer, son of the morning!
Isaiah 14:12

Mouth ajar, Wisdom stared between her Maker and the angry mob at His feet. What was happening? It had only been a few days since she had left to watch over her beloved creatures in the garden. Now she had returned to absolute and utter chaos.

Hatred. Anger. Fear. Rage. Wisdom had never experienced the feelings swarming her brothers and sisters before, but she knew instantly what each were as they assaulted her senses.

She snapped her mouth closed and turned to Love.

All of heaven was in an uproar, yet her Maker sat observing it all calmly, the epitome of power and glory.

A snarling voice invaded her thoughts as she tried to absorb every new sensation at a rapid-fire pace.

"I will exalt my throne above yours! Your days as ruler are over, great and mighty king," Lucifer mocked. "I will do a better job than you ever did!"

She turned. Spittle flew from Lucifer's mouth as he ground his teeth in anger.

Wisdom stared in horror at the growing crowd of angels behind him, all with their fists raised in defiance of her King—*their* King.

"My Lord," Wisdom whispered, anguish filling her soul. "Do something, please."

Love reached out and clasped her hand gently, releasing it after the shortest moment.

"And what are the accusations brought against me?" bellowed the Most High.

The ground trembled and shook, angels on both sides falling on their faces before Him. Wisdom stayed on her face, her silent pleas for mercy fleeing from her being with all of her might.

Lucifer stumbled from his knees to his feet.

"You do not allow me the same power as yourself!"

Accusations hurtled out of the mob.

"You think you are better than us!"

"You demand we worship you constantly!"

"You do not give Lucifer the respect he deserves!"

Wisdom's face flew off the ground.

"Prudence? No…"

Her sister stumbled beside Lucifer, her face contorted by rage. Her fist lifted, she shook it as she screamed against her lord.

"You are not fair! You favor certain angels and treat them better than others, giving them the best gifts. What kind of god are you?"

"Prudence." Wisdom mouthed the word, but it did not find her voice. She grasped the hem of her Lord's garment. "My Lord, my sister!" she cried.

As the vilest of false accusations were flung against Him, the King bent and cupped Wisdom's cheek in His hand. Wisdom leaned into His touch, soaking in His strength. He held her gaze, and her eyes widened.

"Oh my Lord," she whispered in agony, the glimpse He gave her of the future throbbing an agonizing beat in her head.

The Maker straightened.

"Enough!" The Lord Most High stood, all of the angels falling to the ground in His presence. "All of those who have lifted themselves against me this day are to be cast out of heaven, never to dwell in My Presence again."

Gasps and cries of horror reverberated around the throne room. Those with Lucifer looked to him for assurance, panic evident in their eyes.

Michael and Gabriel rose to flank their Commander.

Lucifer picked himself off of the floor and leered at Him, hatred pouring from him in waves.

"We shall see about that!"

With a cry, he pulled his sword, which burst into flame, and ran straight for his creator. Michael intercepted him.

Angels quickly pulled swords from their scabbards, and, with a mighty crash, the first war of the heavenlies began.

Fire clashed and spewed as swords met.

Standing on the edge of the great chasm between heaven and the worlds below, Aurik lifted a blaspheming angel high above his head and turned to look back at the King. At His nod, Aurik hefted the angel over the side and into the abyss below.

"Wisdom, are you with us?"

Her head snapped up at Michael's voice. With a firm nod, she clasped the sword offered to her.

She gripped the soft handle with both hands and wrung it, her heart squeezing that she was about to use a weapon against her Master's creations. Her brothers and sisters. She barely had time to wonder if she could cut down one of her own when an angel barreled toward her, screaming, face twisted in unnatural fury.

Calm overtook her as steel rang against steel. She easily parried and thrust the angel aside, catching another's blade with her curved sword.

She shoved the enemy's weapon away and slashed at the attacking angel. A thin red line beaded along Abundance's face.

Wisdom's eyes widened, and she froze. She had spilled her Maker's blood. The same blood that ran through Him, that He created within His angels—the very blood the creatures below now carried within themselves—she had spilled.

Abundance swiped at her cheek and stared at the stain smeared across her hand.

"You."

The single syllable carried more rage than Wisdom dreamed

Abundance could possibly know.

Abundance swung and swung, each slash accompanied by a hissing grunt. Abundance's blade nicked Wisdom's wrist. Abundance pulled back with a wide grin.

"Not so untouchable now, king's favorite?"

Wisdom glanced at the gaping wound briefly, satisfied to see it close upon itself and the skin smooth out. She turned her full attention to Abundance.

Abundance's eyes widened, and she touched her cheek. Her wound ruptured further, blood tracing red trails down her face.

She snarled and attacked. Wisdom fought her off, heaved her overhead, and hurled her over the heads of the fighting angels. Abundance dropped over the side of the battlefield and disappeared.

Wisdom walked with determination across the vast throne room, gaze swinging in every direction. She thrust aside every blade that careened toward her as she searched.

Tossing angels riddled with hatred out of sight, she briefly glanced at each face, locking into memory each friend she would lose this day.

As she defended the honor of her Maker, she scanned the open room, her stoic face not betraying her racing heart within. Her sister was still on the battlefield. Somewhere. She had to be.

Finally, she spotted her.

"Prudence!"

Her sister spun to face her, her mask of anger slipping for a moment. Uncertainty flickered through her demeanor.

"Prudence." Wisdom dropped the tip of her sword and held out her hand. "Please, come with me, my sister, my friend. It isn't too late to humble yourself before the Maker and repent. Please."

Fury replaced doubt, and Prudence shoved her sword toward Wisdom's chest. Wisdom took a half step back, narrowly escaping the razor-sharp edge.

"Oh, yes, I'll do what Wisdom says; she's always right. Listen to Wisdom; she can't make a mistake. Wisdom. Wisdom. Wisdom. I am sick of hearing your name, sister!"

The two angels circled each other, Wisdom keeping a sharp eye on her sister's movements and the blade inches from her own chest.

"And I am sick of your being at the master's side constantly. Maybe *I* want to be the new master craftsman who the lord delights in daily. Maybe *I* want to be the one everyone turns to when they need advice. Maybe *I* want to be the best!"

"Prudence..." Wisdom warned.

Prudence turned to the King and shouted.

"Did you hear me, king? I will now be the best, the number one craftsman beside my master, Lucifer!"

But the King was speaking to Lucifer.

"You will be known as Satan, the deceiver, for you have deceived many today and turned them away from me. Be gone from My presence!"

White-hot power hit Satan, and he flew back, falling from heaven like a comet.

The King focused on Prudence.

"And you will no longer be called Prudence, but Folly. Be gone from My sight."

He made eye contact with Wisdom briefly before turning His back.

Folly's jaw went slack, and her sword clattered to the ground. Wisdom rushed forward and hefted Folly above her head. She spoke fervently to Folly as she walked toward the edge of the battlefield.

"Remember this always. I cast you out of heaven this day because you slandered the name of your Maker. You cursed the name of the Almighty and worshiped Lucifer as god instead of the one true God. I will forget you after this day, but I am quite certain you will remember me for all of eternity."

With a mighty heave, Wisdom threw her sister out of heaven.

Folly plummeted, barreling toward the blue and green globe far below her. Her face remained impassive, full of shock. Until she hit earth's atmosphere.

Wisdom fell to her knees when Folly's face twisted in agony.

Folly's mouth opened in a silent scream, the pain too much for her to bear, the rate of descent too fast to catch her breath. Fire consumed her, and her beautiful wings shriveled and disintegrated, powdering off of her body like sparkling dust.

Tears slipped down Wisdom's face as Folly fought against the fire destroying her. Wisdom tracked her descent until she crashed into the side of a mountain, tunneling deep within the earth's crust.

Folly lay in a crumpled mess in the hole, unconscious.

Arms hugged Wisdom tightly, but Wisdom could not tear her gaze away to see who held her.

"Our sister," Discretion whispered.

Both angels stared down at their sister, oblivious to the other defiant angels going through the same, agonizing process.

A resounding cry shook the ground, and the remaining rebellious angels were thrust out of heaven as one.

Wisdom turned to look at her King.

The Lord God Almighty, Maker of angels and men, dropped His head and wept.

Chapter Four

You became filled with violence within, and you sinned; therefore I cast you as a profane thing out of the mountain of God; and I destroyed you, O covering cherub, from the midst of the fiery stones. Your heart was lifted up because of your beauty; you corrupted your wisdom for the sake of your splendor…and I turned you to ashes upon the earth…you have become a horror.
Ezekiel 28:16-19

"How many did we lose?"

Gabriel shook his head sadly.

"A third."

The words barely penetrated Wisdom's mind as she stared after the fallen angels, smoking trails curling from each fiery descent.

"So many."

Wisdom turned at Discretion's voice.

"Our sister…"

"I know."

"Oh, Discretion, maybe I should have warned her about Lucifer sooner! I saw her fascination with him. If I would have guarded her better, watched over her more…"

"It is not your fault, and you know it."

Wisdom's face crumpled.

"Yes. Oh, I know she made her own choice, but how I wish she would have listened to me!"

Discretion wrapped her arms around Wisdom again. Wisdom stared at Folly, too still in the crater that held her in its cruel embrace.

"Now I have to forget her," she whispered. A hiccup followed a sob.

"No."

Wisdom glanced at Discretion, surprised at the fervor in her voice.

"Don't ever forget. Don't ever forget the agony of losing our sister. Don't ever forget the cost of rebellion." She dropped her voice. "Remember and be wiser still, sister."

Wisdom nodded, gazing back at the globe, tears tracing silent trails down her cheeks.

"Perhaps she will turn back to the Maker yet," Discretion whispered.

Wisdom heard her sister's low words and sucked in her breath.

Could it be...? Could Folly repent—come home still?

"Wisdom."

She spun around at the word from her Maker.

"Guard My creation, Wisdom. They need you now more than ever."

"Yes, my Love."

Wisdom bowed, and, whirling, quickly kissed her sister's cheek. Vaulting into the air, she flew swiftly toward the new earth and her Master's garden.

❁ ❁ ❁

Folly groaned and curled tighter into herself. What was this agony wracking her body? Why did everything hurt so?

Closing her eyes tight, she tried to fall back into the oblivion of seconds before.

Images rushed her mind, denying her rest. She sat up, screaming as her skin stuck and peeled onto the rocks under her. Her wails of pain quickly turned to cries of outrage.

It was *his* fault. *He* had done this to her.

She raised her face to the barely visible blue above her, peeking through the cavern's gaping hole.

"Curse you!" she shrieked. "I will curse you all of my days!"

She dissolved into sobs and tried to stand. Giving up after falling again and again, she curled into a ball and wept.

"Curse you," she whispered, trying to give into a rest that never came.

❀ ❀ ❀

Folly blinked owlishly and swatted away the hands grasping her. Why did they have to be so rough? She gasped and bolted upright as a sharp slap stung her cheek. With wide eyes, she stared at Abundance. Or, who used to be Abundance. Could that possibly be Abundance?

"Get up, fool. I don't have time to carry your sorry hide around all day."

The snarling and distorted creature could *not* be Abundance. The charred face made her nearly unrecognizable, as did the sneer. That was completely new.

"What are you staring at? You don't look so hot yourself, you know."

Folly blinked. She tried to make her mind understand the wholly new tone of voice. Directed at *her*.

"Uh, sorry, I think. What's going on? Abundance, right?"

Abundance growled and raised her hand. Folly flinched, certain she was about to get slapped again. But Abundance dropped her hand and fisted it.

"Of course I'm Abundance. How stupid are you? Now shut up and listen. The master wants to have a meeting."

"The master…"

"What, did you hit your head a little too hard there, princess? Lucifer doesn't like to be kept waiting." She pointed to the darkness behind her. "Go down this tunnel, turn right, left, then right again, and you'll come to a giant cavern. Lucifer said to move it."

Oh. *That* master. Folly fell back with a sigh of relief, not paying attention to the directions. Shame and indignation warred within her as she remembered her curses to heaven above. Or, more accurately, to the *one* in heaven above. She wasn't looking forward to facing that master ever again.

She sat up quickly, pushing past the pain.

Why should I care what he thinks? I'm not under his rule anymore!

She exalted in the freedom she felt. Until the pain tore at her in waves. She tried to distract herself. It would get better. It would. What had Abundance been saying? Oh, yeah. Lucifer. Meeting. Right. She made herself stand, hanging onto the wall for support. She needed to get to Lucifer's side. Stake her claim.

"Help me?"

Abundance snorted.

"You're on your own, sister. I'm not gonna be late."

Abundance pushed past several hovering shadows and disappeared.

Sister.

Folly wrenched away from the word that resonated in her head. She was no one's sister anymore. She was Lucifer's alone. And she wasn't his sister. She was his *partner.*

She tried to focus on her surroundings. Darkness everywhere, yet she could still see in a fuzzy, grayish hue. Movement caught her eye, and she froze. Straining to see who was in the room with her, she nearly shrieked when a shadow moved from one wall to the other. Her voice trembled, but she tried to sound brave.

"Who's there? Come out. Let me see you."

But the phantoms hovered just out of reach.

Panic overtook her, and she struggled to move forward. Toward them, but hopefully also past and away from them.

She hung onto the jagged wall that burned both cold and hot to her touch. What in the world? What kind of rock was this? Where was she? She got closer to the milling shadows. They drew back, still between her and the black hole in which Abundance had disappeared.

"Move," she growled as she tried to claw her way to the doorway. She wasn't going to be intimidated by, well, nothing. If she couldn't see anyone, then no one was really in the room with her. And she would keep telling herself that until she made it to—where did Lucifer say to meet him? She groaned, wishing she would have paid more attention to Abundance than her thoughts. The milling darkness mocked her bravery, and she tried to hurry. She gasped with each step she took.

The forms took shape as she inched closer. Still out of sight, but definitely present. She caught glimpses of their faces if they came close enough, but she could tell they were trying to avoid her. She stopped and gazed at them. Another ducked away from her sight.

"Whatever. I don't have time for this."

She strained to see wherever it was Abundance had gone. Her eyes burned with the darkness. It hurt so much. She blinked rapidly, trying to adjust her eyesight. She would get used to it, this unnatural dark. She had to.

Making her way out of the room, she stumbled over the uneven ground as she felt her way along tunnels that twisted in endless confusion.

Just when she thought she would scream in hopelessness, an enormous cavern opened before her. Her eyesight cleared. Torches with blue flame flickered against the walls, surrounding multitudes of angels. Two large beams of garish light across the yawning room drew her gaze.

She huffed a relieved breath when she saw Lucifer on the other side of the room.

"Lucifer," she called.

Her words croaked out, not penetrating even to those closest to her. The burns on her face and body throbbed, begging for attention. For relief. She couldn't feel her wings.

She started forward but stumbled when she realized the masses of angels surrounding him were bleeding. Burnt. Skin jagged and torn. Bodies twisted and warped. Moaning in agony. Folly's jaw dropped. How were they even standing?

"But, Satan…" an angel loudly objected.

"Lucifer!" he bellowed. "My name is Lucifer! Just because that… that…*king* said otherwise in no way means I must bow to his wishes. You will call me *Lucifer*."

His fist came down hard, and the angel dropped to the ground, covering his face against further attack. Lucifer sank back into a coarse throne of solid rock. Folly blinked. Where had the throne come from? How long had she been unconscious?

"We cannot attack anytime soon, thanks to your ineptitude." Lucifer glared at the angels closest, accusation seething from his face. "So we will do the only thing we can. For now."

He stood and circled his hand in the air. A hazy fog emerged and grew in size. He snapped his fingers, and Folly cringed against the light.

An angel stumbled into her.

"Hey!" Her eyes popped open, and she shoved him roughly. "Watch it."

Other angels crowded her, trying to escape the bright white invading their dark sanctuary.

As Folly's eyes adjusted, she could make out the two creatures playing in the creator's garden. Her lips turned down in a pout. Why on earth was he showing them this? She was sick of anything to do with the master.

"We cannot attack the throne room, so we will attack *them*. Yes, the maker's precious creatures will have no idea what hit them."

Folly cringed at his unattractive, mocking voice, even though she agreed with his words. Where was the smooth, irresistible Lucifer of before?

"We will attack them so hard, so furiously, rip everything the master has given them away, that they will turn away from their *maker*." He sank into his throne and seethed, gripping the stone arms until blood drizzled from his fingertips. He stared above their heads, eyes unfocused and crazed. "He may have won this battle, but he will not win the war." He bit out each word and flung it from him.

Folly trembled at the back of the room, afraid to come any closer. Who was this monster in her god's place?

He straightened, his eyes snapping to an angel near the front.

"You. Go see who defends the garden. Report back immediately."

"Why her? Why Abundance?" an angel whined. "Abundance..."

Lucifer cut the angel off, pounding his fist on the black throne.

"Abundance? Abundance? Who is Abundance? No, her name is

now *Famine*. From this day until eternity." He turned to Famine. "You no longer bring life and wealth and fullness, but you will wrench all goodness away from the king's creatures until they can no longer breathe. Wring them dry, until they curse his name." He turned back to the offending angel. "If I hear you call her Abundance again, *you* will answer to *me*!"

Lucifer's chest heaved, his teeth bared as he snarled in the angel's face.

Angels cowered before him; fear, new and completely real.

It immediately accosted Folly's senses. She tracked the tendrils pervading the room. A being stood near Lucifer, a thick haze surrounding him. Folly strained, but could not tell who hid behind the cloak of terrifying feelings.

Each tendril snaked from him toward those present, and each angel it connected with trembled and cried out. Folly gasped as a strand touched her. The new sensation swirled in her belly, making her want to retch. Its metallic bitterness soured her tongue. She gave in and vomited from its putrid stench.

A mournful keen from the entity swept through each angel present. Folly bent over, hands clasped over her ears as terror grasped her heart and squeezed. She straightened, ashamed and scared and wanting to go home more than anything she had ever wanted in her life.

Lucifer waved his hand and captured their attention once more.

"Dismissed. Come back when you have some good ideas for me."

Lucifer stood, covering his wince gracefully. Smoke curled from his wings and shoulders.

He paused, his eyes riveted on Folly for the first time. His lips curled in disgust as he looked down at her.

"Do something to make that one look better."

Folly's heart dropped as shame swept her face, its flush lost under the charred skin. All she wanted to do was hide. She yearned for the admiring glances from before. Before this—hell.

He turned to leave, angels clearing a hasty path. Stopping, he glanced over his shoulder at his throne.

"Make it bigger."

As he swept from the room—his limp clearly visible to Folly—angels rushed to the jagged throne, tearing it down with their bare hands. Folly stared between the scrambling angels and Lucifer's retreating back. She thought she had known him so well. How wrong could she have been?

Moans and wails rose as angels cried out in despair and pain. More blood appeared on the hands ripping apart the throne, and makeshift tools appeared in wounded hands as they pounded at the stone, a new throne slowly emerging from the never-before resistant rock.

Folly jumped as boney fingers clawed at her. She jerked away, but they persisted.

"Stop it. Let go of me! Stop!"

They tugged her back down the path she had come, heedless to her cries. Forced onto the bed she had crawled from a lifetime ago, hands belonging to formless shadows pinched and accosted her. A nasty, thick cream was smeared on her bare skin. She felt like she had been set on fire.

She gagged and looked up at the closest angel's face.

Healing stared at his task, his mouth a grim line.

"Who are you now?" she choked out.

"Death."

He roughly flipped her on her stomach. She cried out.

The bones in her wings crackled as Death untwisted them. She started screaming and didn't stop until he was done. Ooze dripped from her wings as he lathered potions on the burnt skin stretched between the bones. Folly vaguely wondered if feathers would ever grow again, then wondered why she even cared. She just wanted the pain to cease.

Task done, Death left without saying another word.

The apparitions swarmed her, peeling away charred skin, smoothing her features, sewing gaping wounds, causing unbelievable agony.

Realization soaked into her as her mind fired with unwanted thought.

Was this her life now?

What had she given up?

What had she done?

Chapter Five

"Behold, the man has become like one of Us, to know good and evil. And now, lest he put out his hand and take also of the tree of life, and eat, and live forever"— therefore the Lord God sent him out of the garden.
Genesis 3:22-23

Wisdom paused at the edge of the garden, scanning the horizon. Sweet magnolia tickled her nose while a gentle breeze caressed her face. She smiled.

Just like the Master's touch.

Glancing over her shoulder, Wisdom sought the keepers of the garden.

Woman sprawled on her stomach in the middle of a field, a large blue and silver butterfly clinging to each splayed hand. Adam swung onto a horse. Whispering in the horse's ear, Adam urged the horse toward his wife at a full gallop. Startled, Woman looked up, the butterflies taking flight. Adam and the horse circled her, then the horse reared. Hooves sliced the air. She cheered and clapped, and the horse dropped back to earth. Adam leaned far over the horse, hand outstretched.

A monkey jumped onto the horse's rump from a tree above and slapped it, pushing Adam from his precarious position in one swift motion. Adam tumbled on top of his wife, and the horse bolted while the monkey screeched and chortled. Adam jumped to his feet and tore after the animals, Woman's laughter ringing after them.

The horse thundered past, skirting Wisdom with a shake of his mane.

Wisdom laughed as Adam surged past the horse, easily overtaking the animal. They slowed, and Adam gave the horse an affectionate pat and spoke to it a moment before turning away. The monkey jumped onto Adam's back.

Adam jogged toward Wisdom, the monkey dangling from his shoulders. The horse grazed far behind him.

"I love how fast Horse is! Did you see that? I almost wasn't able to pass him, but he wasn't about to run faster than me." Adam beamed with pleasure.

Monkey placed a leaf on Adam's head. "You wouldn't have passed him at all had I not been on his back."

"Be nice," Wisdom scolded as she disentangled the monkey from Adam's arm, lifting it to the branches above.

Adam's eyes sparkled as he stared up at Monkey.

"Oh, is that so? I guess we'll have to have another race then. Just Horse and me. Would you care to watch and tell us who's faster?"

"It would be my pleasure," said Monkey as he languidly peeled a mango and sucked the juices from the fruit.

Woman skipped toward them.

"Did you see the race, Wisdom? Isn't Adam fast?"

Woman grinned in delight and gave her man an admiring glance. Adam ducked his head as a flush crept up his neck.

"Yes, he was, dear one. God made him perfect indeed. Don't forget, tonight I'm going to teach you about the Andromeda Galaxy. Maybe we'll even visit it. Sound good?"

"Oh yes!"

"Yes, please!"

Wisdom chuckled as their voices chimed together, their faces lit with the same eager anticipation.

"All right. Enjoy yourselves, loves. I'll be around!"

Wisdom gave them a huge smile and a wave, then glided back to the garden's perimeter. She scanned the horizon again, satisfied there was no unaccounted movement.

It had been weeks and none of her fallen brothers or sisters had come near the paradise.

But she wasn't about to let up her vigilance.

Changing direction, she meandered through the thick foliage at the garden's edge, keeping part of her attention on Adam and his wife.

Cool liquid bit into Wisdom's ankles. She looked down. Clear water gurgled by and she wiggled her toes, enjoying the refreshment. She shook her head and smiled as she thought of Discretion. Discretion would love it here if she would just brave the flight.

Climbing the bank, she froze while clutching a vine, tendrils of black hair wafting across her face in the gentle breeze.

An unfamiliar whimpering noise tugged at her heart.

Checking behind her, Wisdom was satisfied to see that Adam and Woman were kneeling beside a perfect little lamb, tufts of snowy curls making the spotless creature even more adorable. Woman whispered in Adam's ear. Adam roared with laughter, and she grabbed her stomach, doubling over with giggles. They were quite safe.

Wisdom crept forward. Pushing her thick hair out of her face with one hand and parting the leaves with the other, she peered through the branches.

Folly sat on a boulder outside of the lush greenery, her back to Wisdom. Her shoulders heaved and shook as she whimpered.

Wisdom stared in pity at her wings, leathery and claw-like, crumpled in on themselves, where gorgeous, downy wings used to be. The once-creamy shoulders were dry and flaky—grime caked to them. Her fiery red hair was singed short, and, even from a distance, the putrid odor of burnt skin and hair stung Wisdom's nose. The horrendous sight held Wisdom captive.

A slight breeze ruffled the leaves, and Folly turned, looking straight at Wisdom. Folly gasped when their eyes met and dove behind the boulder.

Wisdom stood motionless, heart breaking. Her sister's lovely face was almost unrecognizable. Translucent skin, rippling with scars, clung tightly to the delicate bone structure, giving her a skeletal look. Folly's skin was the color of ash; Wisdom doubted a flush would be able to touch those cheeks again, so void of life they were. Her vibrant purple —sometimes green or orange—eyes were now a murky gray, dull and lifeless. But worst of all, fear, decay, and hatred clung to her sister's shrunken frame instead of the peace and pure joy from before.

Wisdom tried to steel her weeping heart, but couldn't. The pitiful noises continued, softer now.

"Pru—" She straightened, authority bleeding into her posture. "Folly. Come here."

Folly immediately obeyed, trembling. She slunk near the ground, crawling on her hands and knees.

The sight tore Wisdom. As Folly hung her head past her shoulder blades, Wisdom shuddered. The blades looked like they would pierce the skin at the slightest provocation. Wisdom's first response was to speed away for Healing, but she remembered he was no longer in heaven. Because of Lucifer. Satan. No, because of his own rebellious heart. She squared her shoulders, determined to be strong.

"What are you doing near the garden? You are not welcome here." Wisdom's commanding voice echoed off of the surrounding hills and bounced back to them.

Folly sighed and hung her head, her wings crackling with the movement.

"I was trying…trying to remember. Absence from the maker's presence is such torment. Oh! If only I hadn't—but no, it's too late."

Wisdom strained to hear the muffled words, struggling with her desire to hold Folly tight in her arms.

"Too late for what, fallen one?"

Folly blew out a gentle breath and raised her head. Their eyes met.

"Too late to repent."

Folly's expression crumpled, and Wisdom glimpsed tears before Folly fled.

Joy leapt like a flame in Wisdom's chest.

But, oh! It is never too late to repent, dear one!

Wisdom surged into the air and snapped her wings wide, charging after her sister. As she tried to follow Folly's erratic flight pattern, her heart sang within her.

Can you imagine the pleasure on my Lord's face when I bring back one of his precious angels? My sister?

Folly disappeared. Slowing, Wisdom carefully searched the terrain far from the garden. Lush and lovely, the land bloomed with promise. The creatures would adore the home the Maker had made for them when the garden had grown too small for their numbers. Wisdom pictured the best places for them to build their houses. If they wanted houses. Most of them would probably choose to live outside. Buildings were unnecessary, but entirely too much fun if one was a craftsman. Movement caught Wisdom's eye. Wisdom pulled herself back to searching for Folly.

Wisdom spotted Folly hunched against a tree, charred fingers swiping at the sooty trails down her face.

She's fast for having wings that look like they're about to snap in half.

She eased to the ground behind the weeping figure. Wisdom reached for her sister, but the wind blew the gut-wrenching stench in her face and she pulled back.

"Folly."

She spun around, shock and fear stilling the tears.

"You—you followed me!"

"Of course." Wisdom smiled and forced herself to sit next to her sister. The putrid smell was unbelievable. Her entire being protested being near such decay. "It is never too late to repent, darling. Go to Him. Tell Him you are sorry. He'll forgive you; I just know it."

"Oh, I couldn't!" Folly jumped to her feet and whirled away.

Wisdom stood and placed her hand on the raw and peeling skin of Folly's shoulder, but Folly winced and jerked away.

Wisdom's hand scorched, but new skin quickly replaced the melted. She stared at the handprint seared onto Folly's shoulder. She hadn't meant to hurt her, but...

Folly clenched and unclenched her fists.

Wisdom frowned. Was she struggling with pain? Or...or...anger?

"He would never forgive me for what I did. Never."

Folly faced Wisdom once again. Wisdom's knitted brows eased. Folly's countenance wore only sorrow and repentance.

"Of course He'll forgive you. I know He misses you. I miss you. Discretion misses you. Please come home, my love."

Time froze. Wisdom waited, holding her breath, waiting for her sister's decision. Hoping with her entire being.

Folly tilted her head, a smirk tugging up the corner of one split lip.

"You're sure he'll forgive me?"

"Oh, yes! Completely."

"Do you think he'll forgive you?"

Confusion clouded Wisdom's expression for an instant as Folly pointed over Wisdom's shoulder.

Wisdom spun around. Her eyesight flew across the miles, and she easily saw the woman lift a piece of fruit to her mouth, take a bite, then hand it to her husband.

Wisdom's stomach knotted.

"You...you distracted me."

Folly threw back her head, laughter pouring from her.

"For once not so wise, eh, sister?"

Tears clogged Wisdom's throat, and she slowly pivoted toward Folly.

"Never again, do you hear me? Never again will you distract me from my task."

Folly crossed her arms and leaned against the rough bark of a tree. Victory surged on her face.

"Doesn't matter now, does it? Damage has already been done." She grinned. "Go console your beloved creatures in their disobedience." She cocked her head, mocking, feigning puzzlement. "Or will you cast them away like you did me?"

Wisdom hurtled off the ground toward her charges.

Her heart screamed within her as she barreled toward the garden. She had failed. She had failed her Master. She had failed His most prized creation.

Folding her wings, she plummeted to the ground next to them.

"Adam, what have you done?"

Nothing.

She stepped closer.

"Why have you disobeyed the Maker? What have you done?"

The fruit lay on the ground next to them, and they looked at each other, panicked.

She stepped closer and reached out her hand. It passed right through them.

"No..."

Wisdom's blood turned to ice as evil laughter filled the air.

"How's the maker's little pet, today? Having a bit of a rough day, are we?"

Wisdom slowly pivoted and saw Satan standing next to a serpent, stroking the cunning snake's head.

She swiveled away, her back to him. She spread her wings wide, blocking his view and keeping herself between the creatures and the fallen one.

"You're...you're *naked*."

Wisdom's eyes widened as she stared between the man and woman. What did they mean? Adam's eyes dropped, and an expression she had never seen before filled his face.

Wisdom blushed and looked away. Lust. She wasn't sure how she knew, but she did.

"Adam! Stop it! We need — I need, something to cover myself — to cover up. Hand me those leaves, quick! Shut your eyes! Don't look!"

Woman ripped a vine from a nearby plant and started stringing giant elephant ear leaves together. She made a robe of sorts and dropped it over her shoulders. Adam still hadn't quite recovered.

She started on a second garment.

Wisdom watched them in astonishment. What did they mean they were naked? The Lord had made perfect coverings for them, just like he had the animals. Why were they veiling themselves?

And they were acting so strangely. Blushing, stammering, not looking at each other. What had the fruit done to them?

"Here."

The female Adam thrust another robe at Adam and helped him tug it over his head.

"There. That's better. Oh, Adam, what are we going to do?"

"I don't know."

Gasping, Adam grasped his wife's hand and yanked her deep into the foliage of a nearby bush.

Wisdom stared after them with her mouth parted. Was he...was he...*hiding*? Didn't he know the Maker could see right through the trees?

Satan took a step forward.

"Here's the part where they die!" he crooned to the snake, not bothering to mask his giddiness.

Wisdom stood firm, keeping herself between Satan and her charges.

"They have died today, Satan, but not in the way you were expecting."

Wisdom's heart thundered at her Maker's voice. He had slipped into the paradise as the sun began its nightly descent. Her pulse pounded in her temples even as joy sprang in her heart. Tears slid down her cheeks, and she struggled with her desire to throw herself at His feet.

Love rubbed away a trickling tear as He passed her. She peeked up at Him.

Sorrow and compassion filled His eyes.

How she longed for the day—not very long ago—where His eyes held nothing but smiles and laughter.

He stood before the place where the man and woman were hiding, and His voice drifted to them on the breeze.

"Where are you?"

His quiet voice pulled her from her own sorrow, and she straightened to attention.

Adam trembled as he emerged, clutching the hastily threaded leaves to himself.

"I h…heard your v…voice and was afraid because I was n… naked, so I hid."

His words tumbled and fought for dominance. Wisdom's brow furrowed. Adam had never had trouble speaking before.

The Lord frowned.

"Who told you that you were naked? Have you eaten from the tree of the knowledge of good and evil?"

Movement from Satan drew her attention.

"You. Stay."

The Lord pointed one commanding finger at the retreating serpents. Both stood rooted to the spot.

Wisdom twisted back to the creation and their Creator. Their conversation swirled around Wisdom. It was all she could do not to wince with each new pronouncement from the Lord.

"In pain you shall bring forth children."

Woman sobbed, her hands covering her face.

"Cursed is the ground for your sake."

Adam stared at his feet, tears dripping onto his chest.

Except for Satan's. His curse was a tad on the light side. Wisdom would have obliterated him if she were the one handing out judgment. Her heart skipped a beat.

Everything the Lord does is perfect, she chided herself, determined never to rebel, not even in her thoughts.

"Oh, my Lord! It is too much for me to bear!" Adam cried as he threw his hands over his face and wept.

The woman dropped to her knees, keening and wailing till the sound filled the garden.

Love gathered them to Himself and held them until their tears lessened. He kissed each of their foreheads and, veering away, strode toward the lamb grazing nearby.

Wisdom craned her head and watched Satan slink out of the garden. She took comfort in the Master's promise that Satan would remain defeated, no matter what he threw at the Creator's precious creatures.

Woman gasped, and Wisdom spun around. Wisdom gagged and grabbed the nearest tree for support. The perfect little lamb lay bloody and gory on the ground, stripped of its skin.

Wisdom's chest rose and fell as blood pounded in her ears. The Maker meticulously scraped fat from the skins, rubbed salt on them, and dried them. Rubbing an acidic mixture on them, He once again dried the skins and stretched them tight. Threading a bone needle with lamb-gut thread, He sewed together two simple garments.

Wisdom took a deep breath and straightened when the Lord stood and walked back to them. He tugged the leaves free and dropped the new clothes over His creatures' heads.

Wisdom could see the exceptional craftsmanship. The leather was soft and supple, the creamiest of whites. As Adam and his wife fingered their garments, the King turned and walked away from them.

Two more Lights appeared in the paradise, and Wisdom plunged to her knee, dipping her head in respect.

"They are like Us now, knowing good and evil."

"We can't let them stay. They may eat from the tree of life and live forever like this. There would be no chance for redemption."

"It would be pure torture. Agony."

"Agreed. They must go."

Two of the Lights faded from sight, but the King returned to the man and woman.

"You must go, never to return."

Adam and his wife nodded, shamefaced. Woman stared between the lamb and her clothes and squirmed, her face a greenish hue. She fingered the soft clothing and tugged it away from her skin.

A sentry with a sheathed sword walked toward them and motioned with one hand toward the east entrance.

"Wait." Adam took a deep breath and pulled his wife close. "I have one more task." He took Woman's chin gently into his firm hand. "Your name is no longer 'Woman,' but 'Eve,' because you will be the mother of all living, no longer the only woman. I love you, and I am so, so very sorry."

Eve nodded, tears thick in her lashes.

"Me too."

The cherubim's sword flamed to life, and he nodded toward a break in the hedge surrounding the fertile land.

Adam wrapped his thick arm around Eve's slim waist, gently leading her from the garden.

Eve turned around before the ground dipped out of sight, casting one longing glance back at paradise, but the flaming sword blocked her view.

"Eve."

Wisdom tasted the woman's new name on her tongue. It was strange, different, but it worked.

Her heart squeezed as she watched the two leave the only paradise they had ever known. The landscape surrounding them shriveled and the ground hardened, but the garden remained as lush as it had always been. Storm clouds gathered in the distance, the very planet weeping for what had just happened. Eve trembled as she heard thunder for the first time. The ground dipped, and they were lost to Wisdom.

Wisdom stared after them long after they had disappeared from her sight.

Chapter Six

The Lord is merciful and gracious, slow to anger, and abounding in mercy.
Psalm 103:8

Folly turned from side to side, admiring her new, leathery wings.

The skin stretched tight between the bones, not a feather in sight. Burnt off, all of them. She nodded in satisfaction. Their ebony color suited her. She moved her wings gently, the ache deep in the bones just starting to subside. Where her wings had snapped from impact, giant claw-like protrusions sprang from the top of her wings where they had mended—thanks to Death. He said it made her look formidable. She quite agreed.

She turned her back to the mirror, gazing over her shoulder.

She liked them, she decided. She liked them very much.

The others weren't as lucky. Lucifer told Death to help only those who would be the most useful.

Folly snorted.

In a battle, they all would be useful. But she wasn't going to be the one to point that out. No, most of her fellow inmates healed slowly, their broken, twisted bodies slowly morphing into the most hideous creatures she had ever seen.

Lucifer, his skin peeled again and again, had returned to some of his former glory. Some. Those scars would never quite go away, no matter how hard he tried.

Death's skin, charred black, stuck to his bones, his eyes glowing white. Folly had no clue why, but he was by far the worst-looking in the place. He looked like a walking cadaver. When Folly asked why he hadn't used his ministrations on himself, he had shrugged. Said he liked it better that way.

And Lust, well, Lust was something else. Folly thought her own regime was ridiculous—it was nothing compared to Lust's. Lust did everything Death suggested to put herself back together. She wanted to be beautiful like the female creatures.

Folly shook her head, annoyance flaring.

Fascinated with the creature's affection for each other, Lust experimented with ways to twist their love—to make them long for others they shouldn't. She wanted to see how many ways she could hurt them through their love for each other.

Folly was still trying to figure out where the lowly messenger angel had come from. She certainly hadn't been in Folly's circle of acquaintances in heaven. Not that Folly had bothered getting to know the several billion angels in heaven before her fall from grace.

But the worst part of all? Lust was after Lucifer. She was determined to get his attention, no matter what.

Folly ground her teeth.

Well, she would just see about that. Lucifer was hers, nobody else's. A familiar voice caught her ear. Her head jerked away from the looking-glass in Death's chamber.

He was back!

Folly pushed away the constantly picking and prodding fingers and surged toward the entryway. She rushed toward his sweeping figure.

"How did—"

She sprawled on the ground, head throbbing in sudden pain. Lifted straight off the floor, feet dangling, Folly cringed as Lucifer's sulfuric breath blasted her face.

"Tell me, Folly. How do you think it went? Did it go as you expected?" He shook her, his fingers digging into the tender flesh of her arms. "What. Did you take a little nap instead of keeping Wisdom away?"

"I didn't—"

He slammed her against the wall and released her. She crumpled to the ground. Sitting up slowly, she stared at him with wide eyes. Why was he so mad? She did exactly as he asked. Stuffing pleading and excuses far inside of her, she gave him a bored look.

"I take it it didn't go so well," she intoned drily.

Folly dabbed carelessly at her swollen lip and stared at the blood trickling down her finger, ignoring his heaving face. She would take another beating before she let him know how much his cruelty wounded.

A low growl escaped his throat.

"No thanks to you."

His boot slammed into her midsection.

Gasping in pain, Folly curled into a ball as his footsteps echoed away. Her heart squeezed, the pain in her heart nearly crippling. She thought she had done well. She thought he would be pleased.

"Fear! Come here."

The thick, rotting blanket hovered nearby. Clawed toes peeked out from under the cloud.

"Go to the man and woman, wait for her to be with child, then torment the hell out of her. I don't want her just to feel pain; I want you to compound it. Make her think she's going to die. Go. Now!"

The talons clicked on the black rock of the tunnel past Folly's head. Folly vaguely wondered who Fear had been in his past life. Come to think of it, Folly wasn't sure if Fear was a "him" or a "her." Huh. Heavy footsteps thundered back to her. She folded into herself but found herself hoisted off the ground again.

"Let's see if we can give you a task you can't mess up."

Lucifer thrust her toward two shadows who clutched her arms, digging their boney fingers into her flesh.

Fear's never-absent essence tried to enter her heart—she could see the tendrils snaking their way toward her—but she blew them away, refusing to be invaded by that faceless monster.

Blood oozed down her arms, and she swiveled her head side to side, trying to figure out who was dragging her. It was a game she played every time she roamed her new home to keep from going insane. She studied the faces on either side of her. They were so shrunken, so gnarled, she couldn't tell anymore.

Was that what Wisdom saw when she looked at her? A rotting corpse?

Folly clenched her teeth as their conversation swirled in her mind. *Repent, indeed. Like I ever want to go back to that place.*

Folly sputtered in indignation then stilled. A catlike smile spread across her face. She would treasure the despair on perfect Wisdom's face. No matter what Lucifer thought, she had succeeded in every possible way.

Failed! Folly threw back her head and cackled. *Wisdom failed! Just wait until her beloved master—*

Folly gasped as weightlessness seized her, and she plummeted into empty space. Her knees then elbows hit hard before she could unfold her wings. Folly looked above her. Lucifer leaned over the dank hole.

"I want you to think about what you've done. When you can tell me your mistakes, and what you can do to improve them, I will be back with your next task. If I can ever trust you again, that is."

Something heavy was heaved over the slight opening, cutting off even the grayish light. Pitch black met Folly's eyes. She blinked, then narrowed her eyes.

"The only mistake was yours," she growled into the dark.

A howl in the distance dropped her to her knees. A rush of fear swept her. She crawled until she met solid wall and huddled against it. Not the answer Lucifer was looking for.

She opened her eyes hours later.

She had battled with fear and lost. It soaked into every pore of her skin until it saturated her. She stood defiantly, trying to ignore the way her heart quaked within her.

Striding to the wall, she ran into it and fell back. She stared up at it in surprise, not understanding. Crawling to her feet, she reached one hand out and ran her fingers along the rock. Her fingers scorched. She yanked them away and rubbed the ice from the tips.

Solid. Unmovable. She couldn't get out.

Terror overwhelmed her, and she sank to her knees. Tearing at her hair, Folly fought for control. A shriek built within her until she could hold it no longer. She screamed and screamed until her shrieks turned to whimpers, then fell to the floor, sobbing in exhaustion.

She couldn't get out. She was trapped. The rock that she should have been able to pass right through wouldn't budge.

Maniacal laughter wafted into the room and bounced off the walls.

Not so prideful now, are you, hated one?

"Oh, Lucifer, Lucifer, I'm so sorry…just…please, let me out. I won't disobey you again, I promise…just…please, get me out of here."

Folly pulled at her hair, tearing great clumps out. The brittle strands powdered in her hands.

I'll come for you. Eventually.

Silence so loud she could feel it.

Folly screamed again. The walls felt tight; the air, putrid, almost gone. Pressure from all sides crushed her like a flower under a stone.

It wasn't supposed to be like this. It wasn't.

She curled into a ball on the floor, trying to block the terror, the absence of voices, the aloneness. The searing heat. The freezing cold.

No rest. No oblivion. Just torment.

❊ ❊ ❊

"But, Master, what are we going to do? We've lost Abundance, Life, Treasure, Healing. How are your creatures on Earth going to thrive without these angels to help them? You said we each had a role to play; a job to do…"

The little angel's hands fluttered as he spoke, his anxiety clear to everyone present. Panicked eyes sought his Maker's. Wisdom could tell he tried very hard to subdue the new feelings.

The King rubbed the small angel's shoulders and shook him gently.

"You are all a reflection of Me. In Me is all abundance. In Me is all life. In Me is all treasure. In Me is all healing. You have all come from Me. In Me, there is no lack. You can trust Me."

The little angel's shoulders sagged, and he sighed in relief.

"Thank you, Master. I needed that."

Worry creased the little angel's brow once more. "But Maker, what about—"

Love raised a silencing hand.

"Enough, Jotham. You can trust Me. Go."

The Lord embraced Jotham, and he fluttered away.

Perfection is of the Lord. A hint of a smile graced Wisdom's face. Even Jotham's own name held the answers he was looking for. She listened to the other angels speak, and the smile slid from her face.

As Wisdom waited her turn, the other angels vied for the Maker's attention, all distraught over what had happened in the garden.

Finally, the King held up His hand and dismissed them.

The noise filtered out of the room as the angels left in a big cluster, their voices echoing in the enormous crystalline chamber.

Wisdom and Love were the only ones left.

Love stared after the departing angels, His hands clasped behind His back.

Wisdom trembled.

What was He going to do to her? She had failed Him. Failed Him in the worst way. It was because of her He had lost the precious treasures of His garden. It was because of her man no longer had the same fellowship with Him. It was her fault.

Tears slipped down her cheeks.

Love turned and looked at her, the sorrow in His eyes matching her own.

With a cry, she sprinted across the room and into His open arms. He stroked her hair and wings gently while she sobbed.

"Oh...Oh, my Lord...I'm so...I'm so *sorry*. I tried...I failed...it's all *my* fault."

He pulled back and stared into her eyes.

"Can you ever forgive me?" she blurted.

He smiled and wiped one cheek, then the other, with His thumb. New tears quickly replaced the ones He wiped away.

"Oh, Wisdom. My Wisdom. Of course I forgive you. Always."

Wisdom cried out and flung her arms around His neck in a stranglehold.

"Oh, thank You, my Lord!"

Joy warred with astonishment as she marveled at the cleansing feeling that swept through her. How could her Love be so good to her?

He gently tugged her arms away and leaned back to look at her.

"You let your guard down, dear one; something you must never do again."

Wisdom stepped back and ducked her head.

"Yes, Maker."

He lifted her chin with His fingertip until their eyes met.

"Satan is a master deceiver, and he will train his followers to deceive as well. You must always look to Me for guidance, not to them. Do you understand?"

"Of course, my Love. Forgive me."

He smiled.

"I already have. Come. I want to show you your new role for My creatures."

Chapter Seven

"Sin is crouching at the door. Its desire is for you, but you must rule over it."
Genesis 4:7 ESV

Wisdom peeked over Eve's shoulder.

She couldn't keep the silly grin from spreading across her face as the tiny bundle squawked and squirmed in Eve's arms.

Wisdom had watched the Lord construct each part—down to the tiniest detail—of the child while Eve rubbed her belly in astonishment as the mound grew. Now, in her excitement, Wisdom could barely keep her fingers off the newest little creature.

Adam and Eve held each other and gazed lovingly at the little man, enraptured.

"Cain." Eve didn't take her eyes off the little guy as she spoke to Adam. "His name is Cain."

Wisdom smiled as Adam nodded absently and kept staring, like he had been for the past hour. How she itched to hold the small bundle in her own arms!

"May I come in?"

Eve's hand fluttered to her hair, and her gaze bounced around the messy tent. Adam jumped to his feet and bowed deeply.

"Of course, my Lord."

Love raised His hands and stayed their frantic motions. Adam dropped back down beside his wife, peeking at the infant under the soft wool blanket. Eve had worked hard on making the blanket just so. The King caught Wisdom's eye and winked.

A wide grin stretched across Wisdom's face, and her eyes sparkled, beyond excited over the new one. The Master returned his attention to Adam and Eve.

"Peace to you. I've come to see the wee one. May I?"

Eve proudly deposited the suddenly still bundle into the Creator's outstretched arms. Cain gazed into His face, content and curious. They stared at each other, love pouring from the Maker, curiosity and a knowing from the little guy.

Love motioned for Wisdom to join Him.

With a yelp, Wisdom flew to His side, wrapping her arms around both of them. She breathed deeply of the baby's sweet scent, amazed at how delicious new life was.

The child stared between the two of them, finally deciding the Master was more interesting.

"Oh! Isn't he perfect? It was so hard to wait nine months to get to meet him, but it was worth it! Did you see his little toes? Ten of them —can you imagine?"

Wisdom puffed out her cheeks and blew kisses, capturing the child's attention and making him gurgle and laugh. Adam and Eve glanced at each other with delighted grins.

Wisdom stilled and looked at them.

"They still can't see me, can they?"

"No, dear one, I am sorry."

Wisdom stared down at the child, forehead creased, fighting disappointment.

His tiny face puckered.

"Oh! Oh!"

She clucked and made soothing sounds, a soft *brrr* coming from her mouth as she rolled her tongue.

The baby hesitated, then looked back to the Creator. Cain squealed in delight and grabbed a fistful of shoulder-length hair. The Lord smiled, kissed him, and carefully laid him back in his parent's arms. He rested His hand on the child's forehead, and Cain instantly drifted off to sleep.

"Rest, Eve. You have done well."

Eve nodded and snuggled her baby. Adam draped his arm across both of them as he lay down next to them.

Wisdom followed Love from the tent, her eyes soaking in the peacefully sleeping infant until the tent flap closed. She pointed Káel inside. He moved swiftly to obey.

"What happened?"

Wisdom gave the Maker a quizzical glance. She had a feeling He already knew.

She took a deep breath. The acrid stench of battle stung her nose, and her stomach clenched in remembrance.

"They came from nowhere. We were able to hold them back, but the woman kept letting Fear in. At one point, Adam did too, but he mainly fought with us."

"Yes, I heard his prayers."

"Also, I spoke the words you told me to say,"—she looked at him with questioning eyes—"they understood and followed my directions, but they didn't know I was there. Why is that? They couldn't hear me, yet they seemed to understand."

"Remember what I told you? Your fellowship with them will not be the same, but you can whisper into their hearts, and they can choose whether to listen to you or not."

Wisdom nodded, comprehension dawning. She was still learning so much about her new role.

Wisdom's gaze traveled the scorched countryside Adam and Eve could not see with their physical eyes.

It had been a fierce battle. Wisdom wanted to ask the question beating within her heart, but said instead, "They wanted the child's life."

"I know, and, My love?"

Wisdom's tear-filled eyes lifted to meet His.

"I was here the whole time."

Wisdom nodded.

Of course. I should have known.

But at the woman's first cry of pain, fallen angels rushed them from every side. Wisdom fought earnestly, but her heart cried out for her Lord's deliverance. She thought He had let them fight the battle alone. It wasn't until the squirming infant rested in his mother's arms that the dark beings retreated, and Wisdom could breathe once more.

"How are you doing?"

Wisdom sucked in a steadying breath, willing her voice not to tremble.

"I want Satan defeated once and for all, and I want the fighting to stop." She rubbed her toe in the dirt. "And I miss my sister," she added in a small voice.

Images of Folly burning assaulted her mind. Wisdom had not seen Folly in the skirmish; it both relieved and worried her.

He didn't say anything, but she could feel His comfort drift into her. They both gazed over the torn landscape. The scorched view faded from sight, and lush greenery surrounded them once more.

"Can you see the future, Wisdom?"

Wisdom frowned and glanced at Him briefly. Didn't He know? And what did that have to do with missing her sister?

"I can...see...where a person's choices will lead them. I can see cause and effect in the universe, such as gravity. A planet's velocity and orbit affect the rest of its solar system and the universe at large. I can see...I'm sorry, my Lord, I'm not sure what you mean."

Wisdom felt His laughter before she saw it.

"Simple question. Can you see the future?"

The answer is never so simple, she thought.

He grinned at her. "True."

"Well, um, no. No, I can't."

"I can."

She nodded, feeling foolish even while a million questions crowded her tongue.

"Prudence..." She bit her cheek and looked at Him.

He nodded for her to continue.

"Prudence could. See the future, I mean. Glimpses of it, anyway. Not like You can, of course; but, well, I see what *could* happen. She saw what *would* happen, and it always amazed me. 'Clear as gold,' she would smugly say." Wisdom smiled at the far-away memory. "And Discretion, well, she is always so calm, so trusting. Nothing phases her. Not even that time I put two galaxies in the same orbit, remember?"

"I do." He seemed to be struggling with holding back laughter.

"I don't even know how I made such a mistake. Stars were sliding together—anyway, she said You had it under control, and You did. And I learned so much. She knows You are good and You will do what You say. Then there's me." She peeked up at Him. "Why did you make *me* Your master craftsman? Any of the artisan angels would have been a perfect choice, and they probably wouldn't have made as many mistakes while they were first learning. Or even now."

Wisdom's fists clenched as she thought of Folly deceiving her.

"Oh, Wisdom." He leaned over and gently kissed her forehead. "You will see, dearest one. For now, trust Me. And believe Me when I say, there is no one like you. You are completely irreplaceable to Me. I love you and made you exactly as you should be. Perfect, like Me."

She squirmed, pleased yet uncomfortable. She didn't see. She wanted to. Now.

Discretion would tell her to wait patiently—the Lord's timing was perfect. Prudence would have flippantly told her exactly when she would find out, then waltzed off to do whatever it was Prudence liked to do. Sadness filled her. Wisdom had never known how deeply Prudence struggled with jealousy once Lucifer started putting those thoughts in her head. Why on earth should she? Prudence clearly had the more desirable gift.

Love dropped His arm around Wisdom's shoulders.

"I will send Discretion to you. I think she's just what you need right now."

Wisdom smiled at Him.

"*You* are all I need, my Love, but I would enjoy seeing her." A wry grin turned up Wisdom's lips, and she chuckled. "Discretion flying here. Won't she love that?"

The Master laughed and shook His head before vanishing. She

wrapped her arms around herself and shivered. She could still feel Him, and it was wonderful.

She turned and made her way back to the tent.

❊ ❊ ❊

"Are you ready to come out?"

Folly lifted bleary eyes and stared at Lucifer. She didn't answer.

He strode toward her with purposeful steps and gripped a handful of her hair. Jerking her head back, he leaned close to her lips and dropped his voice.

"I asked you a question, my dear, and when I ask a question, I expect to be answered."

Folly croaked out a feeble laugh.

"Yes, *master*."

She spit on him.

His fist came down on her face, again and again, until his anger was spent. She wrapped her wings around herself to protect herself, but he kicked them until the bone splintered, the leathery skin tore — till they hung, limp, at her sides. He released her hair and backed away. She slumped to the side, head reeling, pulse stuttering. Who knew such pain existed?

He paced before her, running his finger madly through what was left of his hair.

"I didn't want to do that. You know that, don't you? You left me no choice."

Folly gurgled another laugh, blood dribbling down her chin. Excuses. That was exactly what he wanted to do to each angel who had followed him. And it was exactly what he did to them all. Frequently.

Folly tried to make her mouth work, but it defied her.

He paused. Watched her. Came close and bent down, eyes curious.

"What was that?"

She coughed, spraying his face with specks of blood. The look on his face? Priceless.

She chortled until the pain from his fists turned her jeers into

63

uncontrollable screaming.

"I will break you" was the last thing she heard him say before her mind shut down. She retreated into herself, waiting for it all to be over.

❀ ❀ ❀

Someone dabbed at her face with something putrid.

Folly tried to open her eyes, but they were crusted shut. Lifting shaking hands, she rubbed her eyes until she could peel them open.

Healing—no, Death—towered over her, grinning.

"You look awful."

She squeezed her eyes shut. "Thanks."

He finished cleaning her face and rubbed a thick cream into her skin.

"You shouldn't cross him, you know."

Folly peeked up at him, then rolled her eyes. "You think?"

Death shrugged. "Just act compliant. You don't have to say everything you're thinking."

"If I wanted your opinion, I would've asked for it."

Death tisked. He started splinting her wings. She winced but refused to cry out. She would not give him the pleasure.

"I think I'm going to enjoy having you here. You're feisty. I'm glad you joined us, Folly."

Folly choked. "Well, I'm not."

"Hmmm." Death's eyes glistened with unnatural light. "I'll keep that in mind."

Fear slowly crept over Folly until she was drenched with it.

Death helped her sit up.

"Listen to my advice. When Lucifer gives you your next assignment, just take it and don't say a word. You'll thank me one of these days."

Folly growled as she hobbled off the slab Death used for an examination table.

"I'll never thank you. Not as long as I exist."

Death smiled. "We'll see."

❀ ❀ ❀

"He did *what?*"

Tears pooled in Wisdom's eyes as she hovered over the brothers, ignoring the other angels crowding around and murmuring amongst themselves.

Cain scurried away, down the path to the vineyard. His parents' sprawling, terra-cotta house rested in the distance, windows glistening —the peaceful home unsuspecting.

Wisdom followed him in shock, hands trembling and outstretched in silent supplication.

The Master appeared in the pathway before Cain. Anger glittered on the Maker's face. Head down, Cain didn't see Him.

The Creator's eyes touched Wisdom's for the briefest of seconds.

"I tried to stop him, but he wouldn't listen!" she cried out.

Wringing her hands, Wisdom hovered above their heads—lost, unsure of what to do next. The Maker stood firm. Cain glanced up and froze—still as a deer before it takes flight.

"Where is your brother?"

The low voice rippled through the air like a thunderclap.

Cain opened and closed his mouth, panic tightening his features. Thrusting his chin out defiantly, he shrugged.

"How should I know? Am I my brother's keeper?"

The Lord took one step forward and came face-to-face with Cain. Cain shied away and trembled.

"What have you done? Your brother's blood cries out to Me from the ground! How can you say you don't know?"

Cain looked down, jaw clenched.

Wisdom's heart pounded.

Come on, she silently coaxed. *Tell him you are sorry—tell him you did wrong! He will forgive you. He will.*

The King waited—just as He had done with Adam and Eve, Wisdom knew—for the faintest glimmer of repentance. Remorse. Of taking responsibility for his actions. But Cain defiantly met His gaze. Wisdom's heart sank. He didn't think his anger—his actions—was his fault. His responsibility. Just as the choice to eat the fruit had been someone else's fault.

Wisdom stared back at Abel's crumpled body, roughly shoved into a thick copse of low-hanging trees. Abel's spirit stood by, shoulders slumped, face ashen, watching his brother talk with the Lord.

"Cursed are you, Cain! Cursed! You will wander this globe, never finding rest, never finding peace for what you have done. The earth will not yield one solitary green plant for you, and you will be a fugitive for the rest of your days. You will not see My face again on this earth."

Desperation shone through Cain's eyes. He sank to his knees, clutching his head in his hands.

"It's too much! If I am hidden from Your face, whoever finds me will kill me once they hear of my curse! I won't be safe anywhere!"

The Lord reached out and pushed His thumb against Cain's forehead, searing a thumbprint into the flesh. Cain winced but didn't jerk away.

"Anyone who kills you will have seven times the curse I placed on you. Leave My Presence. Go. Now!"

Cain stumbled to his feet and fled, never looking back.

The Master looked to Wisdom, power and authority enveloping His anger, indignation, and grief.

"Escort Abel to My heaven, and take him to the place I had you build for him. I will be along shortly."

Wisdom felt sick. She had thought it would be hundreds of years before Abel moved to heaven. She nodded.

Turning, the King strode to Adam and Eve's luxurious dwelling. Wisdom could see Adam building another room while Eve sang and hung laundry to dry, both blissfully unaware. Wisdom turned her back. She had no desire to see their reaction to the Lord's news.

She held out her hand to Abel, who took it wonderingly. He gazed into her face.

"You are so beautiful!" he blurted.

Wisdom smiled even as a slight blush swept her features.

"I think the same of you. Come."

He kept staring at her.

"I remember you. But how can I? Have I seen you before?"

"I have been with you since your birth, dear one. You have listened to my voice and heeded my words. I have very much enjoyed watching you grow."

He stared at her in awe.

"Have I seen you before?" he asked again.

She shook her head, remembering the fellowship she once had with his parents.

"No. It was only important you see the Maker."

He nodded. Tearing his gaze from her face, he stared after his brother.

"Will he be all right?"

"I hope so, dear one."

He lifted pleading eyes to hers.

"Will I see him again?"

Wisdom paused, looking behind her at the Master.

"I don't know," she whispered, wishing she knew. A place was built for each of the many creatures now on earth. It was up to them to accept it.

Eve and Adam raced toward them, despair sapping their faces. Passing the unseen Wisdom and Abel, they bolted straight for the greenery that hid their son's broken body. Adam cried out and hefted the corpse in his arms. Eve screamed and fell to her knees. Grasping her sloping collar, Eve tore her garment down the middle—the garment the Lord had made for her so very long ago. She wailed and keened, clawing the earth with her fingertips, throwing dirt over her hair and clothes.

Adam shouted until his voice gave out and only the echo remained. Wisdom wrapped her arms around Abel as he stood next to her, weeping. The Master walked up to them and gently wiped Abel's tears from his cheeks.

"They may be mourning now, but there *will* be joy when they see you again, Abel. Count on it."

Abel nodded, still staring at his parents.

Love nodded at Wisdom. Tucking Abel against her side, she unfurled her wings and lifted into the air. Abel clutched her as weightlessness greeted them.

She saw the Creator sink to the ground next to the distraught parents and wrap them in His arms before she looked up, eyes focused on heaven.

Abel stared in awe all around him.

"So this is what it looks like up here."

Wisdom smiled through her tears. If only he knew. There was more. So much more. It would take all of eternity to show him everything.

They broke through the clouds and Abel gasped, staring at the vibrant stars and the white-gold city coming into view. Rainbows glimmered down the iridescent towers rising far above the city gates.

"Wow, would you look at that."

❉ ❉ ❉

Folly hid behind a boulder, heart sick.

Cain had listened to her. It had been so easy. He had listened, and she had played into Death's plan, exactly as he wanted. Her hands curled into fists. Never again. She would make her own destiny. She would not be manipulated by Death, Fear, or Lucifer, ever again.

She heard the soft rustling of fabric behind her and froze.

"Very good. I'm impressed."

Folly rolled her eyes. Death's collected voice didn't fool her. She had seen him dance around Abel's broken body like a drunken sop. Until Wisdom had chased him away. Then he had fled as if the maker himself were after him. Coward.

"You make me sick."

Death was silent for a moment.

"Is that regret I hear in your voice?"

Folly ground her teeth.

"Of course not."

"I see."

Her heart skipped a beat.

"What's that supposed to mean?"

She glanced back at him when he didn't elaborate. He grinned at her. She would have given just about anything to know what he was thinking. She waited, but he didn't say anything more. Death's grin was infuriating. Everything about him was infuriating, actually. She turned away, and, not thinking, peeked over the heavy rock she hid behind.

The creator's eyes met hers. She jerked away and fell backward. Scrambling to her feet, she bolted, straight back to the home he had made for her torment.

Chapter Eight

"I have killed a man for wounding me, even a young man for hurting me. If Cain shall be avenged sevenfold, then Lamech seventy-sevenfold."
Genesis 4:23-24

"You have done well."

Folly flicked her wings out to preen them. The painful crackling reminded her they were nothing like the gorgeous wings she liked to show off before. They also hadn't quite mended from Lucifer's beating. She folded them tightly behind her and instead smoothed the form-fitting leather gown she had donned after her heavenly robe had disintegrated. This submissive thing Death had suggested wasn't so bad after all.

"Thank you, master."

Lucifer leaned close, his putrid, sulfuric breath stinging Folly's nose. She discreetly turned her head and took a deep breath.

Not much fresher over here, come to think of it.

"Next time, don't take so long."

Folly's head whipped around.

"It took as long as it was supposed to take! From the first thought of jealousy planted in his heart to the murder—it happened exactly as I saw it." She leaned close and poked his chest with her finger. "Maybe *you* should back off and let me do my job."

Silence.

Not a fallen angel stirred; all eyes riveted on the pair.

Folly forgot to breathe.

Lust slid off Lucifer's lap and slinked away. Lucifer didn't even notice.

Slowly, he sat back in his towering throne, eyeing Folly with an unreadable expression. His hands rested loosely on the clawed arms of the black throne.

Folly forced herself to stand strong—not break eye contact. She told herself she didn't care anymore. She was done being cowed by the abusive monster. She was done being told what to do—done being beaten. If only the rebellious tremors snaking through her body believed her.

His hands stayed relaxed. Folly took it as a good sign.

"All right." He nodded thoughtfully. "What is your plan?"

Folly kept her mouth from dropping open by sheer willpower. *He* was asking *her*? She shot Death a triumphant smirk. His gaping smile didn't change. Raising her chin defiantly, she turned her focus back to Lucifer, tilting her head to show a degree of respect and gratitude. Her voice purred.

"There is a man, Lamech, with a temper like Cain's. No self-control whatsoever. He doesn't listen to the lord, and Wisdom has had no success with him. I think—no, I know I can frustrate him and antagonize his explosive temper." She shrugged carelessly, flicking a piece of ash from her bare shoulder. "Who knows? The wrong person pushes him at the wrong time, and Death can enter the world just a little bit more, robbing the maker's precious creatures of their long and full life." Only this time it was on her terms, not his.

Folly picked at her jagged nails, making herself breathe normally as she waited for Lucifer's response. Her fingers trailed and caught on a sharp edge, the raw skin tearing slightly. She winced and wished for the hundredth time that her nails would grow long and sharp like Lust's. Then again, the girl didn't like to get her hands dirty.

"Folly, look at me."

She took her time lifting her eyes to his, keeping the bored expression on her face.

"I look forward to seeing what you can do."

Her heart pounded in her chest, but a smile creased her scarred face.

"You already have."

She turned and sauntered away.

"Oh, and Folly?"

She stumbled to a halt. Fear hammered in her temples, but she lazily swatted the tell-tale mist away, keeping her back to Lucifer.

"You had better be right. I would hate to be you if you fail."

Cackles filled the air as her fellow inmates jeered at her.

Folly swallowed hard and forced herself to take calm, nonchalant steps from the chamber.

Ducking around the corner, she gasped for air. Fear enveloped her, coating her throat, nose, lungs—skin. She angrily pushed it away, but it clung to her, not letting go.

She was suffocating.

But she couldn't die.

Rolling her head upward, she stared at the black rock, envisioning the too-bright sky above. How she would welcome death, if the opportunity ever arose.

✡ ✡ ✡

"I thought I would find you here."

Wisdom jumped at Discretion's soft voice. She dropped the pillow she was clutching. It landed on Prudence's reclining couch. She smoothed the pillow, her hands lingering on the velvety softness.

"Doesn't seem the same without her," Discretion mused.

"No, it doesn't," Wisdom agreed quietly.

Their gazes traveled over the sparse room. A violet reclining couch, a full-length looking glass, and a few luminous strategy games made of crystal were the only things in the room. Wisdom tugged both pillows straight then folded the light blanket. Nestling it between cushions at the foot of the couch, she stepped back, beside her sister.

"Is it done then?" Discretion asked.

"It is."

Wisdom thought of the field of grass where Lucifer's opulent mansion had once been. The house had imploded with a snap of her fingers, just like every other fallen angel's dwelling. As new creatures were born, mansions would be designed and built for them throughout heaven. Wisdom had gone over the numbers again and again. She would never run out of space for the Maker's creatures, not with the void the fallen angels had left.

Now for Prudence's room. She had come back to it time and time again but hadn't been able to bring herself to do the same thing she had done to Lucifer's residence—make it cease to exist.

"Come. Sit."

Wisdom trailed Discretion and lowered herself on Prudence's settee. She fingered the soft blanket.

"Do you want to talk about it?"

Tears pooled in Wisdom's eyes as she shook her head "no."

"I'm here if you need me."

Wisdom nodded her gratitude. She used the blanket to dab at the tears escaping her eyelids. She started speaking without realizing it, her grief pouring forth in words.

"I don't think I can do it, sis. Destroying every other fallen angel's home was like tearing off a piece of myself. I don't have anything left. I can't lose this part of Prudence, too. I can't. It's all I have left of her. Why did she have to—?"

Wisdom shook her head, covering her face with the purple cloth. Discretion reached for her hand. Wisdom clutched it fiercely.

"Don't you think it's been long enough?" Discretion murmured softly. "You've kept this dwelling long after the others were erased. It's been hundreds of those earth years you're always so fascinated with."

Discretion nudged Wisdom with her shoulder as she tried to tease a smile from her.

Wisdom attempted to smile, but her lips stayed curved downward. She shook her head.

"I'll never be ready. You don't understand. It's like losing our sister all over again."

Discretion stiffened. "I'm hurting too, you know."

"Oh, Discretion. I know. I'm so sorry. I spoke without thinking.

Forgive me."

"Of course."

"I see what she's become, and it makes me so angry—at Lucifer, for deceiving her. At her, for choosing him over Love. I can be strong when I see her like that. I'm ready to fight. I come here, and I see who she used to be. When I come here, well. It seems all I can do is mourn."

She took a deep breath. Tried to prepare herself. To hype herself up for her task. Failed.

"Am I interrupting anything?"

The sisters looked up. One smiled, one did not.

"No, Master. Please, come in."

The King entered the room, standing next to them. He waited a moment before speaking.

"Discretion, may I have a word with your sister?"

"Of course, Maker." She squeezed Wisdom's hand. "You'll know what to do. When the time is right, you'll be ready."

Rising, Discretion tenderly kissed Wisdom's forehead. Her soft footsteps pattered away, the door closing gently behind her. Wisdom glanced at Love. He stared at the strategy board. Taking a few steps, He lifted a ruby pawn and fingered it.

She waited for Him to speak.

He replaced the piece and removed a diamond one from the second tier.

"I'm sorry about what happened to your sister."

Wisdom's voice caught.

"Me too."

He set the piece on the top tier. A king, ruling over all the other pieces. He turned to her.

"Why haven't you completed what I asked?"

Wisdom's head shot up.

"I—You—what?"

He offered her a half smile.

"My love, I asked you to clear all the dwellings of those who will never enter heaven again."

Wisdom jumped to her feet. Prudence's blanket crumpled to the floor.

"I have, my Lord. They're all gone. I..." She paused, glancing around the room. "Oh." Her shoulders slumped. "I—I can't."

He walked toward her, stood very close to her. Lifted her chin with the gentlest of touches.

"Why can't you give this one to Me?"

Her eyes filled with tears. "You know why, Maker."

He nodded. "I do. But will you do it anyway? Give this to Me, Wisdom? Can you release it into My hands and focus on the task I've given you? My creatures need you."

A tear slipped down her cheek, her throat, into the hem at her neck. She nodded.

"I'm sorry. Yes, I'll do it."

He kissed both cheeks, then rubbed away her tears.

"Do you want Me to stay?"

She shook her head and attempted another smile. He kissed her cheek again and stepped back. She sank onto the settee.

It was some time later that Wisdom realized she was once again alone in Prudence's—Folly's—old room.

Her eyes trailed the room. There was not one ounce of personality in the room. Did Prudence mistrust her gifts so much, she never tried to develop them? Wisdom shook her head sadly. She had never asked. She would never know.

Her sister's favorite blanket caught her eye. Bending, she retrieved it. Folding it once more, she placed it lovingly on the couch.

Standing, she walked around the light purple settee, toward the crystalline door.

Wisdom lovingly ran her hand down the spine of Prudence's reclining sofa one last time.

Straightening, she snapped her fingers. Gone. Every last possession of her sister's—gone.

The gentle breeze of the outdoors teased Wisdom's dark strands. Turning, she strode back into her home, firmly shutting the door behind her. The clear door smoothed out and morphed into the rest of the wall.

Discretion stood waiting for her at the end of the hall.

With a shake of her head, Wisdom—numb—glided to her floating chamber far above their heads. Her reading nook beckoned her. She wrapped her wings tightly about herself and sank into the downy cushions. Curling into a ball, Wisdom stared as the stars danced and changed colors. The star's music twirled around and through her, gently holding her heart.

The sky faded from light blue to deep purple, and still Wisdom stared.

※ ※ ※

"For the love, what are you crying about now?"

Folly kicked a spray of stones at Famine. Famine sat at the mouth of the yawning cavern, weeping and staring at the sky above.

"Think of all we left behind—all we gave up."

Folly rolled her eyes.

"Seriously? That's got you blubbering all over the place? Better watch whom you say that to, or Lucifer's liable to tear up that hideous backside again."

With a snarl, Famine leapt at her. Folly gasped and struggled to get Famine's claws off her throat.

"What do you know? You're still Lucifer's favorite, and you got to keep your good looks. Maybe I should scratch up that pretty face of yours."

Folly's heart pounded. Famine couldn't. Death had just put her back together. And he was losing his healing touch. Lucifer wouldn't look at her twice if she changed into the horror most of the other fallen angels had become.

Releasing Folly suddenly, the hunched over Famine slinked away, settling herself at the mouth of the cave once more.

"You didn't break your back like some of us. Go away. Your face makes me sick."

Staring back up at the sky, Famine started to wail. Folly clamped her hands over her ears and gritted her teeth. The high-pitched whistling shook her to the core.

"Stop!" she cried.

Famine looked over at her with mournful, yellow eyes. Folly groped for something to say that wouldn't set Famine off—or get her jumped again.

"Why don't you return if you miss it so much? I hear the master is the forgiving sort. Why don't you leave and put us out of our misery?"

Famine stared up at the sky.

"Oh, no. He could never forgive me for what I did. Never."

Folly turned to leave.

"He'll never forgive you either. Remember that."

Folly hurried away, shivers running up and down her spine. Wisdom's words came back to haunt her. Wisdom seemed to think the maker would forgive. Of course, that was before Folly had deceived Wisdom and pushed Cain to murder.

Famine was right.

Shoving Famine's words aside, she jumped into the air and propelled herself forward. Crashing into a briar patch, Folly untangled herself and leapt into the air.

She barreled into a stream this time, then looked behind her. The entrance to the cave wasn't far enough away to suit her. She shook her head and ground her teeth. She would learn to fly again if it took every ounce of strength she possessed. And the next time Lucifer beat her, he would *not* touch her wings. She would make sure of it.

Standing, she walked the rest of the way, spreading her wings and working the muscles in them. They needed to be strong enough to carry her.

Stumbling over hills and valleys, she smiled when Lamech's tent came into view. He had no idea what was about to hit him.

"What are you doing, daughter?"

Folly spun around, staring open-mouthed at the creator. She stumbled back from his blinding purity and hunched over, trying to withstand his presence.

"I'm—I just—I am—" Folly shielded her face with her hands. *I have no idea what I was doing.*

He stood there, reading her thoughts, examining her secret plans, pitying her. Folly felt exposed. Guilty.

"Are you sure this is the path you wish to take?"

His voice held so much love.

A slow burn began within her. Like a burst of flame, it all came rushing back. He had done this to her. Crippled her. Abandoned her. She would see him dethroned if it was the last thing she did. Hatred seethed within her. She would see each of the master's creatures destroyed and laugh at his heartache. She would make him pay.

She tried to lift her chin but failed. "Yes. This is what I want. I know what I'm doing. I know exactly what I am doing."

His silence hit her harder than any words he could have spoken.

Sorrow like she had never experienced before overcame her, and she fell to her knees in the soil. Tears streamed down her face, and she gasped for breath. Wiping the tears away, she stared at her trembling hands.

What is wrong with me? Why do I feel like this?

Another wave of remorse hit, leaving her panting on the ground.

"Do what you must. But, daughter, know this. Every action of yours I am watching and recording, and every word you speak I am listening to. You are never without Me, no matter how hard you try to escape."

She covered her head with her arms and trembled, the rocks biting into her tender flesh.

The guilt and shame gradually lessened. Slowly, Folly crawled to her feet and looked around. He was nowhere in sight. Longing to run after him, throw herself at his feet, and beg his forgiveness overwhelmed her. She took a stumbling step forward.

Fear assaulted her, wrapping her in its cruel embrace. She struggled to escape the loathsome beast, but it held her tight.

"Don't think I won't tell Lucifer about this," it hissed.

"Let. Go. Of. Me."

Folly stumbled back suddenly, falling hard on the jagged rocks. Fear stood over her, regarding her. Rage boiled inside of Folly. Had Lucifer sent Fear to watch over her like she was some errant child? She stumbled to her feet and faced the obscured phantom.

"You have no idea what I was about to do, Fear! Leave me alone or I'll tell Lucifer you were trying to keep me from my task."

Turning, she stomped away, toward Lamech's dwelling once more. Famine's words pounded with each step.

He will never forgive me for what I've done. He will never forgive you either. Remember that.

She was right.

The maker would never, ever forgive them for what they had done.

A tremble coursed through her. It was too late to turn back now. She had a job to do. And she didn't dare disappoint her god, too.

Chapter Nine

And the Lord was sorry that He had made man on the earth, and He was grieved in His heart.
Genesis 6:6

"But, why? Why must You destroy them, Lord? They are Your loves, Your creation—the work of Your hands! I love them as You do. If you could just—"

"Wisdom, surely you have seen the wickedness flooding My earth?"

"Well, yes, but—but isn't there something we can do? Something *I* can do? If You would open their ears to me, let them see me, maybe I can convince them of their wrong. Maybe I can—"

"Wisdom. Come here."

Wisdom snapped her mouth closed and hurried to His side. "Yes, Love?"

"Look. What do you see?"

Wisdom scanned the globe below her. Emotions flitted across her face. She grimaced and smiled, choked and laughed, clenched her fists and sighed. A tear slipped down her face, replaced by a dazzling smile. So many wonderful and horrendous things happening at once all over the planet.

Her roving gaze snagged and remained on a cluster of people below her. Encircling a man's neck with rope. Stringing him in the treetops. Because he was from a different clan.

"Do you not see why I have to destroy them?"

"But if we—" she whispered.

"Look. Look, Wisdom, look. And see."

Wisdom studied the teeming life covering the Lord's planet. There were so many of them. Surely He couldn't be serious.

A mother bundling her newborn baby, tears in her eyes, caught Wisdom's attention. Wisdom smiled. Precious little one. Her inspection lingered a few moments before moving on.

Two men argued over a piece of land. One turned his back, gesturing wildly at the half-erected stone fence marking the property boundary line. The other lifted a loaf-sized rock and struck him. He crumpled to the ground, lifeless. The murderer tossed the stone aside and grinned. He surveyed his new land with pride and walked away, leaving the body for the crows. Wisdom gaped in open-mouthed horror.

A father tossed his son in the air, tickling him and making him laugh. His daughter tugged on his clothes, gibbering—begging for attention. He hit her.

"How many times have I told you to leave me alone? Go cling to your mother's skirts."

He stalked away, lifting the boy high on his shoulders. The young girl sobbed in the dirt while the boy watched her with wide eyes, soaking it all in. Learning it. Memorizing it.

Wisdom's chest ached. Sly movement grabbed her scrutiny.

A stranger led a child into a dark room and bolted the door.

Wisdom snapped her wings wide.

Love stayed her with a touch. He nodded at Vengeance. She barreled toward the earth, sword drawn. Splintering the door with a powerful kick, she drove her sword deep into his belly, tossed the limp body aside, and carried the child out in her arms.

Fallen angels quickly surrounded the man, dragging him—screaming—away.

Wisdom released the breath she had been holding. She tore her gaze away after making sure the child was unharmed. Her heart ached for the soul who would spend eternity apart from his Maker—apart from Life.

A matron stood over a young servant, beating her until welts raised on her arms and blood crested her face. The woman's daughter stood behind her mother, a smug grin on her face. Enjoying it. Wisdom's fists clenched.

She glanced away, and her eyes caught and held the new mother she had first seen. What—what was she doing? The bundled infant flew out of her arms—right into the fire burning hot at the base of a hideous false god.

"No!"

Wisdom jumped into the air even as another angel carried the little one to heaven past jeering fallen angels, who were exulting in the people's godless worship.

The mother backed away, despair sapping her strength. She lay prostrate on the ground in front of the statue, trying to hold back her sobs, trying to tell herself she did the right thing.

"Do you see? Do you see why I am sorry I ever made them? They cast their infants into the fire, worshipping a god of stone who cannot see or hear them. And all the while, Satan stands next to the debauchery and drinks the blood of My precious little ones whom I so carefully handcrafted in their mother's wombs. Look. Over there. Another slave is mistreated, bearing the brunt of his master's uncontrolled fury. I do *not* want slavery, but, even then, I gave them guidelines since they took men and women as slaves anyway. Masters are to be just and kind. Does he look just? Fair?"

Wisdom shook her head, aching for the life that could have been. Before Adam and Eve's disobedience.

"No, he beats this man, his equal, and thinks he is above his brother. He thinks he can take My place as Master. And over here, a man ravishes a woman who isn't his to enjoy. See how she cries for help? How they pass by her and jest? You see all I see, Wisdom; need I show you more?"

"No, Creator."

"They only hold evil and violence continually in their hearts—they have no regard for Me. They do not love Me. Do you see, Wisdom?"

Wisdom dropped her head. She did see. Every single day.

"But, there are those who still call on Your name. What of them?" she asked.

He looked to the slowly rotating globe, and Wisdom followed His gaze.

Enoch sat with his family in front of a campfire. Methuselah whittled on a piece of wood—a boat forming slowly in his hands—as Enoch spoke to his sons, daughters, and grandchildren about the Lord.

Wisdom listened intently. Love and fervor wove its way through Enoch's quiet voice, and his audience listened in rapt attention.

Mighty warrior angels stood around the homestead, keeping watch. Guarding against attack. Several tents dotted the surrounding area since family members had arrived to celebrate Enoch's birthday.

His 365th birthday. Wisdom watched closely, enjoying their camaraderie. He was too young to have his life snuffed out.

Wisdom peeked at her Master. He smiled as He listened to them.

"You can't destroy them, Lord; you can't."

He looked at her, His joyful expression lingering. He nodded at Enoch and his family.

"They would all come live with Me."

"You promised them a long and full life on terra, my Love. Don't do this." Wisdom swept her hand wide. "Think of all the souls who will be condemned."

"They are already condemned. And, they are turning My sons and daughters away from Me."

"And Your sons and daughters are turning a few back to You."

"A few. Wisdom, My Wisdom—why are you fighting so hard for such stubborn people? They turn away from Me again and again."

She turned back to the vibrant planet.

"Because I love them so. They are my greatest delight after You, my Lord."

A pause.

"I love them, too."

"I know."

Her eyes sought His, pleading. "Let this righteous family live on. Repopulate the earth. They will join You in their time. Your creation is incredible, Maker; don't destroy it. Not yet. You said Yourself there has to be a chance for Redemption."

The King nodded, the smile playing about his lips informing Wisdom that the conversation went exactly as He knew it would.

"Very well, dearest Wisdom. I will speak with Enoch."

He stood and made His way to the edge of the crystal palace.

The King vanished and reappeared at the encampment below. Wisdom smiled and leaned closer, always eager to see how His creatures responded to His presence. The little ones cheered and swarmed the Lord, each vying for His attention.

Methuselah shyly hung back but drank in every aspect of the Maker with hungry eyes.

Enoch stood and embraced the Creator. They spoke for a moment —the King ruffling the hair of the closest young boy. He puffed out his chest and jabbed his cousin with his elbow. The girl flushed and jabbed him back. The lad stuck out his tongue. The girl rolled her eyes. Wisdom chuckled and shook her head. Children. So wonderful.

The Maker motioned for Enoch to follow Him, and the two walked into the shrubbery surrounding the path. The brood returned to the campfire's soft glow, each talking louder than the last about the Lord's visit, and who got the most attention.

Wisdom pulled the earth's blueprints from their resting place in the King's chamber. She studied them, quickly going over the changes that would take place if the Lord decided to flood the earth. Terra's topography would alter drastically.

She made a few notes, the light pressure from her finger making ghost-like marks she could easily rub away later if necessary.

Wisdom glanced up from her writing.

Enoch stood in the midst of heaven, gazing at each new color in awe. The Master stood next to him, enjoying his reaction. Wisdom quickly scanned the earth. Enoch's body was nowhere in sight. Her gaze bouncing back to Enoch, she studied his form more closely.

A smile crept across Wisdom's face. Love must have taken him as he was, for he still wore his worn, dust-covered garment. Wisdom chuckled and returned her attention to her crystal blueprints.

She wasn't surprised. She had wondered how long until the Master showed Enoch the heaven they spoke of so often. She'd never seen Him enjoy someone's company more. She eyed Enoch's awed expression and grinned. The King loved to astound His guests.

The Master tugged Enoch out of his stupor, urging him in Wisdom's direction.

"Enoch, this is Wisdom. Wisdom, Enoch."

Wisdom tilted her head. "How do you do? I've enjoyed listening to your talks with the Master. You have done well, teaching your offspring about Him."

A sad look crossed Enoch's face. "If only they all would listen. My son Methuselah and my grandson Lamech seem to be the only ones who thirst for the Lord."

Wisdom nodded. "I understand. I wish all would listen too."

Enoch looked between Wisdom and Love questioningly. "The Lord has told you of His plans — ?"

The King nodded. "Wisdom was informed as well. Anything we spoke of you may freely say to her."

Enoch relaxed. "My Lord, I beg of You one thing. I had no desire to live among the wicked any longer, but my son, Methuselah, does not feel the same way. He relishes his life and Your teachings. He is a man of peace who desires peace and seeks to turn others toward You. Please, please wait to destroy the earth until his years are spent. He is a mild-mannered man who, well, a destruction of this magnitude would overwhelm him. I beg this of You for my son's well-being."

The King nodded once and glanced at Wisdom.

Wisdom stared at the Maker, eyes wide, heart swelling with hope. *Oh, please agree!* she urged.

He smiled at Wisdom but spoke to Enoch. "It shall be as you wish it, My friend. Come. I have much to show you."

As the two walked away, Wisdom sighed in relief. She quickly rubbed away the notes for a redesigned earth.

Maybe—just maybe—when Methuselah entered heaven, her plans wouldn't be necessary.

Wisdom unfurled her wings and swooped toward the vibrant orb.

Maybe—just maybe—she could get someone to listen.

❊ ❊ ❊

Folly sat on a stone wall, roses the size of both of her hands surrounding her. Their thorny vines crept in and out of the stone like overgrown ivy. She sat among them, relishing the silence. The peace.

She eyed the ruins of the once grand castle. It was ancient. Even before its destruction, it had lasted thousands of years. Until Folly.

A family feud had stripped the owner of heirs, leaving the patriarch alone and empty—wondering what foolishness he had fought so hard, so adamantly over.

Then Folly led the giants to him. They ate the livestock right on the spot—Folly shivered. It was beyond grotesque. Then they ran throughout the castle, smashing everything in sight.

The lonely old man took his life before the giants could do it for him.

Folly fingered one of the soft petals. The plant wrenched its petals away from her, hissing.

"Oh, calm down. I won't touch your wretched maker-made petals."

The roses unfurled and settled back onto the rock, further away from her. It seemed like the plants hadn't forgotten their creator, unlike the creatures.

A smile pulled up Folly's lips, but it didn't reach her eyes. Yes, the creatures had listened to her, yet her success tasted bitter in her mouth. She sagged—defeated, tired.

They were close. So close. Only a handful still called on the lord for help. Trusted him. All the rest followed Folly and the other fallen angels with abandon.

Lucifer could smell victory, and it drove him quite mad. Folly snorted. He had always been mad, but she had been too taken with him to notice. Now he pushed Folly harder and harder, not letting her breathe, not letting her have a moment to herself.

Folly's thoughts drifted to Lamech.

She barked a short, humorless laugh. Lamech. What a popular name. The first had caved so readily, killing the first man who had provoked him. This Lamech, however, was impressive. He stood strong against women, drink, idol-worship. She was running out of ideas. Lucifer thought she wasn't trying hard enough.

Her fists clenched. She had gotten nowhere with that cursed Methuselah. God-loving cur. Smiled at whatever came his way and tried to make peace in every situation. Peace! Made her want to scream.

She reached again for the petals. They reminded her of the soft lounge chair Wisdom had crafted for her visits to Wisdom's lofty study. Her hand stopped, rigid.

Hatred filled her and boiled over.

Falling to her knees, she searched among the leaves near the ground. Finding the plant's thick base, she grabbed it and yanked the woody stems from the soil, tearing handful after handful of roots from the dirt. Huge thorns like daggers cut into Folly's palms and fingers as the vines struggled and fought. She didn't care. The pain from her shredded hands pushed her. The last root snapped free, whipping toward her face. She jerked away, but a welt crested on her face. She shook her head to free herself of its sting. The plant screamed then shriveled, lying still.

Tossing the roses from her, Folly stalked angrily away, blood dripping from her hands. The angry welt throbbed.

She was going to smother this ridiculous depression and take out the last two people who truly cared what the maker thought. Methuselah and Lamech.

❀ ❀ ❀

Lucifer stared after Folly's retreating back.

"Imagine that. Lucifer, the great and mighty, scared of a little thing like that."

Lucifer spun around. Death gaped at him in his endless grin, and

Fear hovered to his left. Through the thick fog, Lucifer saw Fear's crossed arms.

Death chuckled. "It's a wonder we follow you at all."

"Why, you!"

Lucifer lunged for Death's throat, only to be crippled by sudden terror. He dropped mid-lunge, grabbing his head. His ending flashed in his mind, many different versions of what could happen when the maker's promised defeat occurred. Lucifer panted, tore at his hair, gnashed his teeth. He felt the crackle of bone as his teeth fought against collapse.

The horror lessened.

Straightening, Lucifer smoothed his tattered cloak and pretended a calm he didn't feel. "I am not afraid of her," he growled.

"Yes, you are. You're terrified. You're afraid of losing her. Afraid she'll use her gift and see your end—turn against you. You're scared she might repent."

Lucifer growled low in his throat but didn't answer. Death continued.

"She is the only one who can help you outwit the maker, and you know it." Death turned to leave, Fear following. "Don't let her know how valuable she is to you, Satan," Death called over his shoulder.

Lucifer clenched his fists and vowed revenge deep in his heart. Revenge against both Death and Fear for making him cower. And Folly, if she failed him.

"Lucifer," he snapped.

"Your name is Satan now. Maker's orders. Get used to it."

Oh, yes. Revenge of the blackest kind.

Lucifer watched them leave, glad to be rid of them. But a cruel question tugged at him. One they could answer.

"What if she fails?" he called. "What if she cannot turn the last of the righteous away from their maker?"

His entire body trembled at the thought. Death took his time drifting back toward Lucifer, eyes on Folly.

"Then your defeat is complete. Never again will there be a chance to turn the entire earth away from the creator, according to Folly. There will always be a remnant if you do not act now. And swiftly."

Lucifer snarled and lunged at Death, pulling himself up short from actually attacking him.

"You stay away from her, you hear? She is mine—*mine*. If you want to know anything she sees, you will hear it from me, understand?"

Death turned his sightless, murky white eyes from Folly's torn wings and rested their chilling depths on Lucifer.

"I understand. Sir."

The tone was mocking, false, but Lucifer would take it. He would deal with Death later, once he discovered Death's weakness. It was unfortunate Death had found his first. Death would soon see who was master. As would Fear.

"Remember, don't let her know, or you'll never be able to use her again. You know how much is at stake." Death's voice faded as he and Fear vanished from sight.

"Don't worry, I won't," growled Lucifer to an empty castle hallway.

If Lucifer had the slightest chance of defeating the creator, he needed Folly. And he hated to admit it.

Chapter Ten

But Noah found grace in the eyes of the Lord.
Genesis 6:8

"You—you mean you won't destroy all of them?"

The King nodded.

"You mean—you mean, I'll get to *speak* to him?"

"Yes." A grin lifted the corners of the Master's mouth.

"He'll actually hear me...*see* me?"

"Yes, Wisdom."

Wisdom whooped and danced around the latest blueprints spread in the King's antechamber. She bumped one. It shifted and started to float away, but Wisdom snatched it and stuffed it back into the pile.

Coming to stand once more before the Lord, Wisdom folded her wings and hands and tried to school her expression, but a grin kept peeking through.

"And what is my assignment, Creator?"

The Maker laughed and shook His head.

"How I love you so, Wisdom. I want you to design a ship and teach him how to build it."

She glanced at the rippling blue surrounding the lush green landmass.

"A ship?"

"Yes, a ship."

He held out His hand, and several ghostly images appeared in His hand. As each ship flashed by, Wisdom assessed their practicality and Noah's ability to build each one.

She plucked a clear pencil from the air and grabbed a blank sheet of glass floating nearby, quickly etching notes. The tip of the writing instrument seared white light into the sheet of crystal, and the shape of a boat rapidly formed. The ink glimmered a rainbow of colors as it settled into the glass.

"I have specific requirements, of course, but the rest is up to you. It needs to hold two of every animal, seven each of the clean, and Noah and his family."

Wisdom paused, her hand mid-air. Her eyes flew to the globe, and she made a swift head count. She slowly looked at Him.

"No one else, Master?"

He shook His head, sadness settling into the lines of His face.

Wisdom gave a quick nod and went back to scribbling, intent on getting his requirements down. Her excitement from moments before dulled. Had no one else even cared to follow Him? After all this time?

"Wisdom."

Wisdom realized he had spoken a beat after the room settled into silence. Wisdom started and jerked her gaze to the Maker.

"Sorry, uh—yes?"

His eyes crinkled at the corners, and He bit His cheek.

A blush crept its way up Wisdom's neck.

"I'll be speaking to Noah when the sun rises, so I'll want your plans before then."

"Yes, my Lord."

Wisdom bowed and hurried from the King's chamber. Beating her heavy wings, she soared toward her perch. Boxes of clear parchment tightly wound into scrolls littered her apartment. Sheets of glass sprawled all over her couch. She seriously needed to straighten her room before her sister made her build stairs so she could do it. Enclosed stairs.

Wait. Her sister.

She glanced down.

Oh no!

She darted behind Aurik's dwelling, clutching her drawings to her chest. She peeked from behind the brilliant white surface.

Discretion waited for her by the front door.

Wisdom fluttered her wings and glided in a wide circle around her home, using other dwellings for cover. Sneaking up the backside of the needle-thin base, she crept to her chamber. Why in heaven's name had she made the whole thing clear anyway? Privacy was never an issue—until now. She wasn't avoiding Discretion exactly—okay, she was. Wisdom sighed. They would just have to talk later. When things slowed down, and, well, when Wisdom didn't feel like her heart would burst with every mention of Folly's name.

Wisdom landed in her study and hurried to her desk, breathing a sigh of relief when Discretion kept staring out the front wall.

Wisdom halted when she caught sight of her desk. Okay, that was just too much. Heavy volumes overflowed from her desk onto the floor. Loose papers stuck out every which way. She tugged one free and stared at it. Research. On the creatures. She eyed the books. She needed to get the tomes back to the scribe's library. Especially since most of the books would be finished soon.

She picked up one and flipped through it.

Each creature had one. The first half of the book—their life's story, as it should be. The second half, blank until it was filled with the story the creatures made for themselves. She snapped the book closed and started gathering those strewn across her desk. Jotham seriously needed to consider switching to the light, one-page crystal books that held the same number of pages or more as the monumental texts. She chuckled. He never would. He liked ink and paper too much. She stacked the volumes into a pile near the edge of her room.

On her way to see the King, she would tell Jotham where they were.

She hurried over to her desk. Pulling blank glass from her stash, she picked up her favorite pencil. Light shot into the ice-like document with each scratch. Another boat formed.

With a swipe of her hand, her glass cleared and she quickly made three more sketches, each different from the last. She scrolled through the options she had made, making sure she had written down everything she wanted.

Satisfied with the rough drawings, she pulled out a much longer pane of glass, hunkering down to make detailed blueprints of each boat. She glanced at her notes. Each vessel would match the Lord's specifications, but He could choose which He liked best. She paused and erased part of her sketch. That technology was beyond Noah's time.

Hours passed.

Wisdom finished the last blueprint and sat back, fully satisfied. She scanned them briefly for errors. None.

Gathering the scattered crystal sheets, she rolled them into a scroll and gently eased them into her pocket. She didn't want them wrinkled before the Master saw them. She darted to the Maker's chamber—making a brief stop to see Jotham—and waited impatiently for His attention.

He accepted the scrolls from her trembling fingers. Smoothing them flat, He grasped the hardened sheets. She watched His face through the scrolls' clear surface, a specter of a boat between them.

She bit her lip when the King glanced at her after scrutinizing the first ship.

"You made the ship very big, Wisdom."

Lip still between her teeth, she nodded once. He continued.

"It will hold all I asked and more—most of the creatures on the surface."

Wisdom clasped her hands behind her back. "All of them, actually, if they don't mind the close quarters."

"Wisdom…"

She held the Master's gaze, eyes pleading. "You said Noah would preach to them until the very end. You said each creature on terra would be given a chance. You said there is always an opportunity for redemption."

The Maker's smile was sad. "If they all repented, My love, there would be no need for the world below to be cleansed."

A sheen of tears coated her eyes. "Please, Maker. Your mercies are everlasting. Prove it."

The King laughed. "You never give up, do you?"

Wisdom lifted her chin. "Not when it comes to my—Your creatures."

"And your sister?"

Wisdom flushed and looked away.

"She deserved what happened to her."

Love gently grasped her chin and turned her face toward His. His eyes held compassion.

"Yes, dearest Wisdom. I want to give them every opportunity to repent. All of them."

A smile like sunshine exploded on Wisdom's face.

"Really?"

"Yes, My love. Really."

She threw her arms around Him, then pulled back after a mere second. She grasped the blueprint and swiped until the third ship came into view.

"Look at this one."

Her entire being bubbled with excitement as the Lord chose and refined her prototype. She carefully made the changes He asked of her and transferred them into several copies for Noah. She bounced on the balls of her feet as she waited for the King to take her to the sphere's surface.

"Are you ready, Wisdom?"

"Am I ever!" she nearly shrieked. She bit her lip and danced in place. "Can we go now? Can we?"

The King laughed. "Of course, My love. Lead the way."

Wisdom snatched the glass papers spread in the King's antechamber and barreled for the earth, crystalline maps and notes and blueprints and sketches springing from her arms, threatening to escape. She just clutched them tighter.

The Creator was waiting calmly for her on the surface.

She grinned and took her place behind Him, waiting for the

moment the Maker would reveal her to his beloved. Noah. Her grin stretched wider. How she had yearned for a moment like this!

Wisdom knew the instant Noah saw the Lord. His entire face lit up, and he ran toward Him. She bit back a yelp when Noah came within inches of her.

"Now, Lord; now?"

"Patience, dearest Wisdom."

She nodded and waited not-so-patiently while the Maker explained to Noah that he had found grace in His sight, all life on earth would be destroyed, but Noah and his family would escape on a craft.

"But, Lord, forgive me…gopherwood? I don't even know how to build a boat. I will do anything You ask, You know I will, but, how do I proceed? What do I do?"

The Creator dropped his arm around Wisdom's shoulders and tugged her forward.

"This is My master craftsman, Wisdom. She is here to instruct you in every aspect of shipbuilding."

Wisdom watched Noah's eyes widen as comprehension dawned. Wisdom grinned. The blinders melted away, and he gaped at her.

"Hi. I'm Wisdom."

Noah threw himself on the ground before her.

"No! No! Get up! You mustn't worship me, only the Maker! Only ever the Maker."

She knelt, scattering off-white parchment everywhere as she tugged him to his feet.

He stared at her with wide eyes and open mouth.

"I am a servant, like you. Now," she smiled. "Would you like to see the plans for your ship?"

❋ ❋ ❋

Folly sagged against the wall.

969 years and nothing. Nada. Not one blasted sin Methuselah hadn't repented of and been forgiven for. Nothing she did turned the peace-loving fool away from his maker.

Folly raked her fingers through her greasy hair, trying to ignore their trembling.

Only one left. Noah.

Folly stared at her quaking hands a moment before dropping them to her sides.

Lucifer hounded her, never giving her a moment's peace, never letting up. And now—now the creature who had consumed her day and night had died. A purely natural death—peaceful, easy. Smiled, closed his eyes, opened his real ones, stood, and calmly went with his escorts to the king's palace. To top it all off, he lived the longest of any of the maker's creatures. Outlived his son, Lamech, and almost outlived his grandson, Noah.

Lucifer was furious. So Folly hid.

She cringed against the wails of the souls in despair. She avoided this section—hated it with everything within her. But she was a tad on the desperate side. A beating? Or the maker's lingering compassion that welled within her at each despairing cry? It was torment either way, and she couldn't decide which was worse.

She sighed. Tried to take a calming breath.

Maybe now that Noah was the only one left, Lucifer would take it easier on her.

She laughed a mirthless laugh. Not likely. The tantalizing scent of victory was driving Lucifer mad. His efforts grew more frantic, more daring. The horde focused all of their efforts on Noah and his wife. They were whipping the creatures into a frenzy against Noah. People ridiculed him, laughed at him, asked to hear about his god only to mock when he tried to explain the creator's mercies.

Folly snorted. Mercies. The "mercies" Wisdom spoke of were a load of tripe. What kind of god allowed such suffering, such violence in his world? The unmerciful kind.

Lucifer would have his victory. Mankind would be destroyed. But then there was Noah.

Folly frowned.

How did Noah play into all of this?

A hint of Noah's path flashed before her. Surging water. A tossing boat. A whisper of the future. Folly trembled, weak as the vision melted away and left her.

Lucifer already knew his time was running short. He didn't need to know what she saw. Victory stood just outside the reach of his grasping fingers, and Folly already bore the brunt of his frustration.

No need to make it worse.

❀ ❀ ❀

Wisdom's feet brushed the clear-gold pavement as she landed at the entrance to the palace. Her feet had barely settled on the glistening surface before she hurried down the hallway that by-passed the throne room. Noah and his family worked endlessly on the "ark," as he called it. It was nearing completion, but the Maker had asked her to join Him instead of creating with Noah today.

Wisdom fairly sizzled with anticipation. She couldn't wait to see what the Maker wanted.

She had spent nearly a hundred years assisting Noah—a lengthy audience with the King was most welcome. Wisdom knocked on the seldom-closed door to the Creator's antechamber and waited.

She frowned.

The Master had told her to meet Him here. Where was He?

"Wisdom."

She glanced over her shoulder. Gabriel hurried in her direction.

"Come quickly. Satan demanded an audience with the Maker. The King wants you to join Him right away."

Wisdom rushed toward the throne room. "Why wasn't I informed?"

"I came as soon as I could."

Wisdom nodded at Gabriel's curt reply and touched his shoulder. She hadn't meant to snap at him. He darted a quick glance at her, and the tension in his face eased. But the concern in his eyes never wavered. Gabriel opened the heavy doors for Wisdom, and she barreled through.

Fiendish laughter and jeers met her ears before the doors were fully opened.

Satan bowed before the throne, a few former Seraphim flanking him, their towering forms only slightly diminished. Leathery wings rose far above the giant angels, but their posturing did not intimidate the King of kings one bit, Wisdom noted.

Indignation quickly replaced satisfaction.

Wisdom's nostrils flared. How dare they enter the throne room!

Gabriel prodded Wisdom in the Master's direction, and she marched to His side, respectfully taking her place near Him. His Son stood nearby, arms crossed, brows furrowed. Wisdom felt a subtle acknowledgment from the Creator, although His eyes never left Satan's face.

"What do you want, Satan, deceiver of nations?"

Satan bowed deeply, his small hoard of followers cackling at his exaggerated face-plant. Satan straightened, collected and self-assured.

"I bring you news, oh great one. Methuselah, your 'faithful' servant—is dead."

Satan paused, looking up at the King expectantly, letting his news soak in.

Wisdom glanced at the Maker too, surprised. She hadn't known. She had just left Noah—had Methuselah left earth in her brief absence?

The Master's stony stare was Satan's only reply. Satan swallowed hard and cleared his throat. Wisdom felt a surge of triumph at his discomfort.

"You tell him, Lucifer," hissed one of his angels in a hushed cheer.

Satan blanched and shot a glare behind him.

"Satan, you fool! How many times have I told you to call me Satan?"

The fallen angel's mouth dropped open, his tittering silenced.

"Anyway," Satan continued, once more to the King. "If you are truly the righteous king you claim to be, you cannot allow this wickedness to continue. Fulfill your promise at the garden, holy one. They ate of the tree of the knowledge of good and evil. You promised death. Now fulfill it."

Satan's smug grin slipped as the silence from the King's side of the room stretched on.

Wisdom gritted her teeth.

Destroy him. Destroy him now, Maker, and be done with it.

All things are right in their time. Remember that, daughter.

Wisdom dropped her head. *Yes, Maker.*

Satan lifted his chin, jaw clenched, eyes hard. "You promised."

"And what is it to you what I do with My creatures?"

Satan's face flashed red. He opened then snapped his mouth closed. After a visible struggle, he kept his tone civil. His eerie calm returned.

"I wouldn't want you to go back on your word, mighty one. The earth is my kingdom, after all, and I demand justice."

Wisdom's gasp echoed in the roomy chamber. Satan speared her with a hateful look.

"Your king gave the world to those weak beings. They, in turn, serve me, and voilà. The earth belongs to me." He turned his attention back to the Lord. "Not one of them serve you any longer, and—since they are mine—I want them destroyed."

"What of My servant, Noah?"

Satan waved his hand in dismissal.

"He's one man out of millions. Millions who won't listen to him, by the way." Satan spread his hands wide. "Bring him to live with you here, if you like. Just get him off my world. You have no reason to deny me what's mine any longer. So, again, I ask you—where is the death you promised me?"

The Almighty, Maker of heaven and earth and all that live above and below stood slowly, His eyes flashing fire.

Angels immediately knelt, including Wisdom, and Satan's two bodyguards flew back, limp. Satan's entourage cowed and inched away, unable to look at Him. Satan fell to his knees but fought for his position, struggling to lift his eyes to the Master's face.

"You will have your death. Get out."

The fallen angels shrieked and fled, dragging the unconscious seraphim behind them. Satan nodded, the crafty smile on his face turning Wisdom's stomach.

"It's been a pleasure. As always."

He turned and ambled from the chamber, once again ensuring all eyes were on him.

"Allow Me to die for them now."

Wisdom's head jerked up at the hushed words between Father and Son.

"No. The time is not right." The King's voice boomed across the chamber. "Michael. Gabriel. Raphael."

The three Seraphim snapped to attention.

"Go break the fountains of the deep. Go slowly—take your time. Give them every opportunity to hear Noah and repent."

The rushing sound of mighty wings covered Wisdom's strangled cry.

The King looked at Wisdom. "Make sure the ship is complete."

"Yes, Master."

Wisdom barreled toward the earth, easily passing the slow-moving Seraphim.

It was happening then. It was really, truly happening.

Chapter Eleven

And Noah did according to all that the Lord commanded him.
Genesis 7:5

"Happy 600th birthday, dear." Noah's wife handed him a small package wrapped in brown paper. "I'm sorry it's so late. I thought with your grandfather's passing, and trying to complete the ark...well, anyway, here you go."

"Thank you, dearest."

The couple held each other in a comfortable embrace and kissed.

Noah's wife pulled back and looked at him. "And you don't look a day over 500."

Noah threw back his head and laughed. "I don't believe you one bit, darling. I didn't have gray hairs until the boys were born. Now look at me." He stepped back and spread his hands wide. "Streaked with gray from crown to beard."

"Oh, hush," she chided. "You're still as dashing as the day I married you, and the gray is only starting to show. You are strong, have three wonderful boys who love you and married godly young women and have been shown great mercy by God, for which I am exceedingly grateful."

He wrapped his arms around her once more, resting his chin atop her head. She nuzzled her youthful face in his muscular chest.

"I am too, dearest. Exceedingly grateful." He stiffened. "Wisdom!"

She stepped forward and held out her hands in a calming manner. A smile crept across her face. She so very much enjoyed watching the creatures' affection for one another.

"Forgive me. I couldn't find it in myself to interrupt. Shall I come back at another time?"

"Not at all. Please, won't you sit?" Noah stepped away from his wife and pulled out a masterfully crafted wooden chair. "Break bread with us, perhaps?"

"No, thank you."

Wisdom smiled kindly at Noah's wife, who tended to stare at Wisdom with thinly veiled awe each time Wisdom came to visit or teach. She had yet to say one coherent word in Wisdom's presence.

"I can only stay a short time." She briefly admired the completed vessel in the distance. "You have done a fine job, Noah. I've come to instruct you in a few things you will need to know after the waters recede. Terra—earth—will change drastically and you need to be prepared. I've also come to say goodbye."

Dismay flickered across Noah's face; disappointment over his dear wife's.

"Must you?"

Wisdom grinned. "Must I instruct you? Surely my lessons haven't been all that bad."

Noah shook his head emphatically, Wisdom's humor lost on him. "Must you go? The ark isn't finished yet."

Wisdom nodded, sobering for his sake. "She's sea-worthy. Add any finishing touches quickly; there's not much time."

The couple glanced at each other, eyes wide.

"How are we going to get all the animals on the boat? Where are we even going to find them?" Noah's wife blurted.

Wisdom smiled at Noah's wife, who blushed and ducked her head. "The Maker will be along shortly to help you with that. I am needed elsewhere."

"I'm sorry to hear that," Noah said quietly. "There is still so much to learn."

Although her heart ached, Wisdom smiled to reassure them. "All you need to know comes from the Maker, and He is never far away. But don't worry—I will always be here to whisper into your hearts the way of understanding. Listen for my voice. The Lord will send me every time you ask for me, but you must open yourself to His voice in order to hear me. Stay faithful. Be vigilant. Your Enemy will be furious to know you have escaped unscathed. Now, here's what you need to know."

* * *

"I have never been so humiliated in all my days!"

"Really. Getting thrown out of heaven the first time did nothin' for ya?"

Folly ducked too late. Satan's fist slammed down on her head, again and again. She tried to fight him off—tried to stop him—but he was furious. Unstoppable. Needed to vent.

The last blow sent Folly across the room, taking out a row of stalactites as she skittered through the air. Her lungs collapsed as she hit the volcanic rock wall, and she slid to the floor, gasping for breath.

Folly lay crumpled on the floor as her lungs begged for oxygen.

Stupid! How could I have been so stupid?

The familiar jeering and cackling was eerily absent. Folly wondered if he were coming back for more. Her vision grew spotty and unfocused. She fought against oblivion.

"Never again, do you hear me? Never! I will soon be king, master, lord in that wretched god's place, and he will never humiliate me again. Folly! Come here."

Folly would have laughed if her lungs allowed her. A stream of air wheezed past her lips, but Folly sucked for more with desperation.

"Bring her to me!"

Clawed fingers gouged the flesh of her arms as they dragged her backward across the rough cavern floor. Jagged rocks tore into Folly's back and leather clothing. She peeked at the blood and black strips trailing behind her before letting her head drop, trying to gauge how close she was to Lucifer.

They deposited her roughly, sprawled, at Lucifer's feet.

He bent down and grasped her cheeks with one hand, forcing her mouth open. His wild eyes came into focus, inches from her own.

How dare he?

Folly jerked her head away, furious and embarrassed. Her lungs pulled in more blessed oxygen. She felt a praise to the creator rise to her lips as her gaze focused. She stuffed it down as Lucifer grabbed her head and pulled it back toward him. Holding her head still, he clutched her face once more.

"What did you see? Tell me exactly."

"I already told you, you worm."

Lucifer slapped her, still clutching her hair.

"Tell me!" he roared in her face.

"Water," she gasped. "Complete and utter destruction."

"Yes! Yes. What else?"

Lucifer knelt before her, eyes desperate. He cupped her cheek with his other hand—the hand not holding her hair.

"Everything is destroyed, right? Everyone—gone. I win. Right?"

Folly started to laugh.

"You fool. There is a remnant. There is always a remnant."

"No! You told me! You told me!"

Lucifer dropped her and backed away.

A laugh bubbled out, then another, until hysteria took over and she couldn't stop laughing.

"Did you really think you would win against the one who created you? Look at your army! It's pathetic. You can't even meet him in battle."

Folly's laugh was cut short by a boot slamming into her stomach.

The kicks and punches came so fast she couldn't protect her head or curl her legs into her stomach. She folded her wings tightly behind her, desperate to protect them. Another kick and she vomited blood. The stream gushed over Lucifer's feet. He cursed and jumped back. Her lungs collapsed with the next impact.

Her world faded to complete darkness.

◊ ◊ ◊

Folly raised her head. Dropped it back down.

Blasted cell.

As awareness slowly took over, she realized she was staring at the floor. Far below her.

Folly rolled her head from side to side. Chains. Clamping her arms to the wall. She fought back fury. What kind of chains could hold her? It was unthinkable! She tugged weakly against them, hoping they would allow her freedom.

She slowly realized she could only see out of one eye.

"Must be swollen shut," she grumbled to herself.

The distorted words didn't match her thoughts. She licked her lips, the many cuts stinging.

"Good. You're awake."

Folly forced her head up, eyes blazing.

"Get. Out."

Lucifer shook his head and strolled around the room, arms folded behind his back. He looked composed, calm—completely unruffled. His clothing was once again impeccable.

"All that hatred. All that fury. It is incredible you have that much spunk after your unfortunate beating."

Unfortunate? Folly writhed more vigorously against the chains.

"You mean the beating that *you* gave me?" she asked, her garbled voice dripping syrupy sweetness.

He sighed. "Dearest Folly, I did not want to, but you forced my hand. Can you imagine the revolt that would ensue if all of my followers thought they could treat me as you do? I admire your pluck —I really do—but we must keep it to ourselves, darling, not let the others know how it is between us."

Folly's heart skipped a beat.

She opened, then closed her mouth. A frown turned her lips upside down.

"How is it between us, exactly?" she asked carefully, intrigued in spite of herself.

He gave her a pitying look.

"After all this time, you still doubt how important you are to me? I cannot do this without you, you know. After our...disagreement...I thought I would ask again. Nicely. Now, tell me, my dear; what did you see of the creatures' end? Leave nothing out, I warn you."

Folly barked a short laugh. "And what's in it for me? Chains? Imprisonment? Another beating, perhaps?"

Lucifer flicked a wrist, and the chains dropped from her hands. "Oomph."

Folly sprawled on the stony sand, mouth full of grime and dry as paper. She spit out what she could and sat up, too sore to do anything more than sag against the wall.

Lucifer nodded to the hole above their heads—the only way in or out.

"Death waits for you with his healing ministrations. You are very fortunate, you know. I do not allow many the use of his black arts."

Folly cringed. Death—formerly the angel Healing—had never been as powerful as Raphael, the Seraphim in charge of the healing arts. But now, it was nothing like before. Death's potions were as torturous as they were revolting. His healing touch sent fire and intense pain shooting through her for only the slightest results. His powers were weakening; his skill, lessening. He now feasted on decay, corruption, and the dead bodies of the maker's creatures.

And any time a whiff of his potions reached her nose, she would double over and heave until there was nothing left. Well past that, even. She wanted nothing more to do with Death.

Lucifer shrugged, oblivious to her aversion.

"Perhaps after you see him, you can join my table. It's not manna, but it's better than the slop the rest of you get."

Folly eyed him suspiciously even as her mouth watered at the mention of manna. How she longed for heavenly food!

She grabbed her head and hunched forward.

She had to stop thinking of her old life before she drove herself mad! Folly forced herself to concentrate on their conversation.

Manna. Slop. Right.

She knew she ate better than the others, and she had wondered if Lucifer had anything to do with it. Another reason she was picked on.

As if the other angels needed a reason.

"You mean, eat with you once? Or from here on out?"

Lucifer picked at his nails, feigning nonchalance. Folly could feel the desperation radiate from him.

"That depends on you, my dear."

Folly straightened. A grin tugged at the corner of her mouth. It was now or never.

"I want to eat with you from here on out. I want the recognition I deserve. *Especially* if you are going to use my insights to help you."

Lucifer stared at her, face blank. Folly took a deep breath and pushed on. Why not?

"And one more thing. I want Lust gone. Put her on assignment somewhere, move her, get rid of her, chain her—I don't care what. She is nothing more than a lowly messenger angel. She doesn't deserve your attention, and she doesn't deserve to be at your side."

Lucifer grinned at her. "Jealous?"

She raised her chin defiantly. "Those are my terms. Or you'll figure out your future on your own."

Lucifer's smug expression slipped.

"Oh, I'm sorry, was I to think you only wanted to know about the creatures' end?" She grinned, enjoying his discomfort. "Don't you wish to know more about the master's words to you in the garden?"

"Hate, Religion!" he snapped, his focus flying to the prison's exit. "Remove her from this place!"

The two angels dropped into the cell and jerked her to her feet.

"Gently, you fools!" His cruel smile twisted his face. "Death awaits, my dear."

Chapter Twelve

"On that day all the fountains of the great deep were broken up, and the windows of heaven were opened."
Genesis 7:11

Wisdom cringed with each sword's powerful plunge into terra's crust. Muscles strained in the Seraphim's necks and shoulders as the earth cracked and ruptured. Water gushed straight up in powerful fountains, spraying geysers. The solid landmass split and shifted. With each plunge, the earth changed shape, water rushing into the crevices created by the swords to form separate landmasses. The heavens filled and boiled, finally bursting with moisture. It rained for the very first time. Wisdom dropped her head and wept. It was too late. The creatures would not have another chance to love the Maker before eternity met them.

❀ ❀ ❀

Lust sashayed across the room and lounged on the arm of Lucifer's throne, displaying all of her…attributes…for the room of fallen angels to see.

Folly gritted her teeth.

Vamp.

Subtle hissing sprinkled the room—Folly was glad she wasn't the only one disgusted with the attention-grabbing whore.

"What news do you bring me, Lust? Good news, I hope?"

Lucifer shamelessly traced one finger up her leg.

Folly's entire being shook as she clenched and unclenched her hands. That she-devil had no right to sit there. Lucifer had promised her—*promised* to get rid of her! What was she doing here?

Lust threw back her head with an affected laugh.

Folly rolled her eyes. Lucifer didn't know a fake laugh when he heard one. Lust couldn't stand the sight of him, but all she had to do was show a little leg and Lucifer didn't care.

"News of the best kind, master."

Lucifer raised a brow, an inane grin stretching his mouth wide.

"It is done, then?"

"It is."

A low boom rattled the floor. Folly barely noticed it.

"The ship won't float?"

A real grin creased Lust's darkly beautiful face. Her blond hair shimmered in the dim light.

"The ship won't float."

Lucifer whooped and jumped to his feet, swinging Lust around in a circle. He let go of her too soon and she stumbled, hitting her back against the throne. She barely kept from falling. Anger and hatred flared on her face.

He turned away from her and faced those watching.

"Ha! There won't be anyone left! There goes the maker's precious remnant."

He speared Folly with a triumphant sneer. Folly would have hit him had she been closer.

He held out his hand to Lust.

"Come, my dear, tell me everything! How did you do it? Will they find it? Did any of the angels see you?"

Three loud *pops* thundered from close-by. Folly glanced over her shoulder, a frown marring her face. Steady plunging and crashing noises grew louder. Lust froze, her fingers inches from Lucifer's, and stared at the rock wall next to her. Swirling and gushing surged from far away. Lucifer looked annoyed while the others gazed at the walls in fear.

Folly stared around her with wide eyes. The crashes came closer—the gushing, louder.

"Famine! Come here."

Folly watched Famine scurry from the farthest corner of the room.

"What in the world is all that blasted noise? I can't even hear myself think!"

Famine trembled and jumped with each new *crash*.

"Forgive me, my lord, but I do believe that is, uh, water."

"Water?"

Lucifer stared at Famine like she had lost her mind.

Folly rolled her eyes even while she couldn't help but think how close to the truth that was. For all of them. She was holding on to the last shreds of her mind with all she was worth. Folly growled low in her throat while Lucifer impatiently waited for Famine to explain.

Infuriating. Was he really that stupid? Did he think the water she had seen was a trifling stream while some other catastrophe befell the creatures? No, when the creator did something, he did it big.

"Yes, sir. Water. It seems the maker has answered your plea for judgment in a rather, um, unconventional way."

A grin crept onto Lucifer's face and widened into a full-fledged smile.

"Excellent. Most excellent. Folly—"

A tremendous *crack* interrupted Lucifer as a rock wall slammed him into Folly. The water surged around them and twirled them apart.

Folly was battered mercilessly within the swirling tempest, her cries swallowed by the angry waters. She slammed into rocks and other fallen angels as she twirled round and round. Spots swam before Folly's vision. A loose boulder smashed into her. She gulped water into her lungs and pain exploded all over her body.

The roaring finally stopped after what seemed an eternity. Folly squinted, staring at the swirling bubbles surrounding her. Water filled the chamber. Completely. Her eyes drifted shut.

❁ ❁ ❁

Shut up. Oh, please, just shut up.

Wailing, screeching, shrieking—it was loud and it was close. The noise surrounded her. Folly's eyes fluttered open, and her lungs burst with pain. Spirits streamed past her, screaming in agony. Folly wondered at the sheer number of them, then squeezed her eyes closed. What did she care about phantoms when she was enduring such torture?

❖ ❖ ❖

A year.

It had taken over a *year* for the waters to recede from Lucifer's lair. And Folly had counted every second.

The entire time, Folly and her helpless companions had tumbled in the worst kind of torment. The water gagged them, choked them, refused them oxygen—but they couldn't die. They could only survive in the worst agony Folly had yet known.

It wasn't until Folly's knees slammed against the ground—and she wasn't spun away by the current—that Folly realized something was different. The water was—gone. Just like that.

Folly gagged and choked, spewing her stomach's contents everywhere. For several days, Folly and her companions lay on the burning rock, vomiting and breathing. Nothing else.

Finally, Lucifer scrambled to his feet and up the winding tunnel to the surface. Folly crawled after him, discovering how to stand again halfway there.

She could hear the others staggering after her.

Lucifer raced out of the pit, pausing at the crest into the valley. The fallen angels tumbled into the blinding sunlight one by one.

"Quiet!"

The horde of tromping feet stilled behind him, a few shoved from their feet by others when they didn't respond fast enough.

Silence stretched on for miles.

Folly strained her ears. The constant hubbub of humanity wasn't there. Gone. Silenced forever.

Lucifer started to chuckle. His chuckles turned to roaring laughter, and he sank to his knees. Gripping the rocky soil, he clutched handfuls and let it stream through his fingers as he arched his back and howled.

Folly glanced quickly to Lust.

Her eyebrows were arched so high they were lost behind the blond hair swept across her forehead. She stared back at Folly in shock, her animosity momentarily gone. Folly was sure her face mirrored Lust's.

Lucifer punched the air with his fist.

"What do you have to say for yourself now, huh? Every one of them—gone. Dead! Was it worth it? Was it worth casting out your most prized being for a few creatures who would last only a handful of years then be swept away?" He stopped speaking and gazed all around him, soaking it all in. "Well, guess what. I'll take it. I'll take this earthly kingdom you've given me and make it mine. I'll make this earth everything I wanted it to be, *without* those puny brutes to get in my way. Thank you for your generous gift." He threw back his head and guffawed. "Famine, Death, Fear! Scout the north quadrant. Religion, Hate..." He continued to bark out orders.

Folly glanced across the barren landscape, young shoots and saplings pushing their way out of the drenched soil. A part of Folly mourned for the creature's lives that had all been snuffed out so... simultaneously.

Where is this coming from?

Folly rubbed her arms, chilled. She turned to Lust.

"Guess you can build one of those temples and keep it all to yourself now."

Lust sniffed and tossed her long, blond hair over her shoulder. Animosity was back. Big time.

"What good will it do me without a mass of worshippers?" She smiled slyly. "Maybe I'll find the garden and take it for myself."

Folly shivered. Lust could have the garden if it still existed. Folly didn't want to live in a place that reminded her of her sister or her first beating. She snorted. What didn't remind her of a beating anymore?

Lust sauntered away, swaying her hips as she walked toward Lucifer.

Folly realized a second too late where she was going and rushed to overtake her. Jumping in front of her, Folly slowed and calmly walked toward Lucifer.

Lust elbowed her aside.

Folly shoved her, hard, but Lust caught herself before she hit the ground.

"Why, you," Lust snarled through her teeth.

Lust wedged herself between Lucifer and Folly and snapped her leathery wings wide, smacking Folly in the face.

Folly grabbed Lust's hair and yanked her away from Lucifer.

Lust shrieked, twisted away, then dove for Folly, fingernails outstretched.

"Enough!" Lucifer shouted. His voice echoed down the valley.

Folly shoved Lust away from her and stood close to Lucifer's side. Lust scrambled to Lucifer's other side.

Lucifer stepped away from them, his disgust apparent.

"Vicious dogs," he muttered.

Lust stuck her tongue out at Folly with a rude hand gesture. Folly clenched her fists, wanting to tear that despicable face off her nemesis. She started toward her to do just that.

"A boat? You found the boat! Where is it?"

Folly's head snapped around at Lucifer's frantic shouting.

"Look for yourself, master."

Lucifer pushed the trembling angel aside. He beat his torn but heavy wings, forcing them to lift him into the air. He gained height slowly. Folly watched, mouth open, as he struggled to stay afloat, his twisted and broken wings fighting for each beat. Charred feathers drifted down with each flap of the once breathtaking wings.

Even broken, wounded, and only a shell of his former self, he was still so beautiful.

His eyes focused in the direction his spy was pointing. Lucifer cursed. Folly's heart stuttered to a stop even as she strained to see what he was looking at. A heavy ship rested on the crest of a tall mountain.

"Go! Now! Report back. Did they live?" His spies scurried away. He looked at the other angels. "Go see if there are any other boats, just in case. Be quick about it!"

Masses fled at his bidding. His gaze trailed across the hordes then froze on Lust.

Lucifer dropped back to the earth, landing with a jarring crash. He carefully folded his broken wings and tucked them regally behind him. He made his way to Lust and stopped before her.

"I thought you had taken care of it," he said in a low voice, eerily calm.

Lust stuttered and shied away.

"I had—I mean, I did, master! There is no way the ship should have survived. I swear it!"

"Tell me what you did. Exactly."

Lust trembled as her eyes darted around her. Her companions either sneered or looked away, not one offering support. Folly almost felt sorry for her. Almost.

"I—I, my girls—temple priestesses distracted him—the son— Ham, I think?—right at the most important part of the task. And he did—I mean, I did—he was so mad—it worked. He left gaps—there were gaps—I swear it—I saw it. The pitch didn't cover—it should have sunk. The craft should have sunk."

Lust blinked furiously, moisture gathering in her eyes.

Folly huffed and rolled her eyes. Tears? Seriously? What an idiot.

Lucifer leaned close, barking out each word. "And when was the last time you checked to make sure these supposed 'gaps' were still in the hull of the ship?"

"That day—a year ago—the day I came to report to you—the day we were swarmed by floodwaters. It was there; I swear it!"

He backhanded her. She fell to the ground with a cry.

"Get out of my sight," he snarled.

"It...it was Wickedness' idea!" Lust blurted.

Folly frowned. *Wickedness? Who on earth and below is Wickedness?*

Lucifer growled. "I don't care whose idea it was. You failed."

He smacked her again.

Lust staggered away as Lucifer kicked and hit her.

"I swear! She said it would work, that it was the best thing to do..."

"I said, get out!"

Lust scurried to her feet and bolted, disappearing into the young trees of the fresh earth.

Folly's shoulders shook with silent laughter. About time! Oh, but revenge was sweet.

Who's our master's favorite angel now?

Lucifer turned away and stood with his hands clasped behind his back.

As Folly studied him, her eyes drifted to his wings. She had thought he held them far above his head to show regal dominance. She never imagined he held them that way because they were permanently disjointed. Death must've not been able to repair them as he did hers.

Folly eased toward Lucifer, pity moving her forward. She longed to comfort him—to be loved in return. Valued, even.

"Lucifer!"

Her attention snapped toward a little angel tumbling over rocks in his haste. He stood before Lucifer, panting.

"You've got to come see for yourself, sir. You just won't believe it."

Fallen angels appeared from all over the globe.

"No other boats, sir."

Lucifer nodded and started walking, his hunched gait breaking Folly's heart. Maybe if he knew how much she cared for him, he wouldn't be so cruel all of the time. Maybe he just needed to know someone was in his corner. Folly just needed to show Lucifer that she really, truly cared.

She smiled as she strode boldly by Lucifer's side.

She would show him how much better she was than Lust.

Climbing out of the bowl-like valley, Lucifer turned to his followers.

"Folly, come with me. The rest of you—stay here."

Folly couldn't help the smug grin she shot Famine, who was already moving to join him. Famine's chest heaved as she glared at Folly. She had been Lucifer's go-to scout since he had established his rule on the earth. She rarely missed details, so hungry she was to destroy god's creatures. Folly laughed. Well, not anymore. Lucifer wanted *her*, not anyone else.

Lucifer walked away, and Folly jogged to keep up.

Once out of sight of the masses of disfigured angels, he once again unfurled his crackling wings. It took considerable effort to lift himself into the air, and Folly hovered behind him, careful not to let him see how much better her wings had healed than his. Lucifer went down often. Folly mirrored his flight path, pretending to have just as much trouble as he did.

Lucifer knelt after a rather painful landing.

"Tell no one," he panted.

"Yes, master. I wouldn't dream of it. I can administer Death's potions later if you like."

His eyes snapped to her face, his words clipped.

"No one touches me but Death."

"And Lust." Folly smiled sweetly at his quick glance. "Perhaps you should have someone look after you who actually cares. Someone who isn't just after recognition from being at your side."

His expression eased. "Aren't you, though?"

She glanced away.

"Help me up this mountain."

Folly nodded, the muscles in her jaw tight, and together they climbed. Halfway to the ship, they came to a gentle slope and heard braying, squawking, and the hum of a few voices. They peeked over the edge.

Folly's jaw dropped.

Noah and his family—his wife, his three sons, their wives, every member of his family—stood around a well-built altar, lifting their hands toward the heavens.

"No, it couldn't be. That's impossible."

Folly trembled at Lucifer's quiet, steely voice. She stayed where she was, refusing to cower—expecting a fist to her head at any moment.

Lucifer opened his mouth, but the presence of the Almighty

dropped out of heaven and His voice boomed across the land.

"Never again will I send a flood to cover the entire earth. This rainbow will be a sign of the covenant between you and Me."

It continued, but Folly turned to watch Lucifer. Hatred clouded his face; he hissed unknowingly at the maker's voice. Forget being strong. She readied herself to jump back at the first sign of violence.

The powerful voice bled into her thoughts.

Folly trembled at the love the maker openly showed for his surviving creatures. She had felt that love once. Then she had spurned it for hate, fear, torment. Bitterness crept into her soul. It was Lucifer's fault. If he hadn't lied to her, she wouldn't be in this mess.

Noah and his family scattered. His sons started digging what looked like a foundation for a large home.

Without a word, Lucifer straightened, turned around, and slid back down the mountain. Folly watched him go with loathing. She hung back, reaching the bottom long after him, hoping he would forget all about her. Hoping he couldn't sense the hatred that grew stronger every second she looked at him.

"Excellent."

Folly stopped. His pleased voice frightened her.

What?

She shied away from his clenched fists. He speared her with a maniacal smile. Fear overwhelmed her hatred.

"As long as the world endures, I will have a chance to kill, steal, and destroy the maker's most prized possession—his creatures."

Folly stood there, dumbfounded, as Lucifer walked away.

He—he wasn't going to hit her? Wasn't he just deliriously happy that the earth was his alone? What was he thinking? What was *wrong* with him?

Folly stayed far behind him as they crept over the rough landscape back to the cavern.

※ ※ ※

Wisdom smiled and turned away. Noah would never know of the gaping hole in the hull of his ship that his son had left, or the Maker's goodness in sending Wisdom to repair it in the midst of the flood. He didn't need to know. The Creator had spared him, and that was enough for Wisdom.

Chapter Thirteen

Now there was a day when the sons of God came to present themselves before the Lord, and Satan also came among them.
Job 1:6

"You are sure?"

"Of course I'm sure. I wouldn't have told you if I weren't. His sons and daughters listen to me. I promise."

"And the wife?"

"Like clay in my hands."

"Do you think the man himself will do it? Curse his god?"

Folly hesitated for the first time.

Lucifer raised an eyebrow. "If I am going to do as you suggest — which I have to ask permission for, by the way — I want certainty. Assurances. Can you, or can you not *guarantee* that creature will turn his back on his creator?"

Folly lifted an eyebrow in response.

"What creature hasn't cursed his god under such dire circumstances? I think the only thing you need to worry about is whether you can get permission or not."

Lucifer didn't look convinced.

Folly took a deep breath. It was now or never. She sidled close to Lucifer and dropped her voice to a sultry purr. Wouldn't Lust be proud?

"Lucifer. Think of it. You, turning a man who adores his maker, one who has no fault in him, away. He will not speak against his creator no matter the circumstances, and for that, the almighty has blessed him beyond measure. What will that do for you? For us?"

She took a deep breath and held it, daring to run her hand across his chest. Move number one in making sure he stayed out of the clutches of Lust.

His eyes darkened. He grabbed her wrist, pulling it away from his chest, and tugged her closer. Folly bit her lip against the pain his tight grip caused and closed her eyes. Maybe he would kiss her like she had seen the creatures do when they held each other in affection. Lust, after all, mimicked their moves with Lucifer every chance she got. Folly both craved and despised his attentions, but right now she needed him. Whether she wanted to or not.

His laugh took her by surprise. Her eyes flew open.

"Very good. You're learning more than I thought."

Fury lit inside her and she jerked away, but Lucifer held her tight.

"Listen well, young Folly. You don't want to play this game. And, when you do, you'd better be prepared for the consequences."

He shoved her away and stalked toward the door.

Folly's heart sped in her chest, and she shook her head to clear it. She called after him before his cloaked figure disappeared in the inky blackness.

"Consequences?"

He paused.

"Ask Lust sometime."

And he was gone.

Folly stared after the powerful figure that had vanished from sight. Rejected. Again. Would she never learn?

❊ ❊ ❊

Wisdom stood beside the King. She had arrived early to make her report, and curiosity held her later than she normally stayed. The earth had repopulated quickly, and she wanted to see how the princes of the earth fared. And she wanted to hear their reports. Each angel oversaw a different region of terra's surface, and they kept their charges safe from the attacks of their unseen enemy. Unfortunately, very few of the creatures fought alongside the sons of God.

The ruling angels lined up, each presenting themselves to the Maker. A darkly cloaked figure caught Wisdom's eye. She stared. The King acknowledged the angels, then glanced at the figure at the line's end. He walked toward the fallen cherubim.

"Satan. Where do you come from?"

He glided forward, each movement a shadow of the grace and poise he possessed before. A crafty smile slid onto his face.

"From roaming to and fro upon your glorious planet."

"And what do you think of it? Of My creatures?"

Satan shrugged, looking bored. His eyes wandered from the Maker's face to the swirling clouds on the globe below.

"I think of the planet much as I did before. It could be so much better without a certain plague infesting it."

Wisdom clenched her fists and stepped forward. How dare he call the Maker's creatures a plague? The Creator circled the room and touched Wisdom's shoulder, offering her a reassuring smile. His gesture calmed Wisdom, but how she would love for Satan to disappear from one word from her Master. For good.

It's coming. It's coming. That day is coming—whatever it holds. Any way Satan is defeated, I will take it.

"There *is* a certain creature…"

Satan paused and glanced at the King as if asking permission to continue.

Wisdom glanced sharply at Love. Couldn't He see what Satan was doing? He was baiting the Master, pure and simple. But why?

Of course I see it. Relax, Wisdom, My love.

Wisdom took a deep breath. Of course. She focused on Satan's next words. Which of her dearest creatures did Satan wish to attack now? It was rare he asked permission. It had to be somebody important. Someone the Lord protected. Someone…no. It couldn't be.

"Have you seen My servant Job? In all he does, he praises Me above all."

Wisdom's head snapped to the Maker. What in heaven? What was He doing?

A grin spread across Satan's features. Wisdom could very nearly hear him think, *That was too easy.*

Satan barked out a static laugh. "Praise you? Of course he does! You bless him, make everything easy for him, protect him from my angels—of course he's going to bless you. Take everything you've given him away and he will curse you to your face. He only praises you cause he doesn't know the meaning of the word *hardship*."

Love smiled. "We shall see. What do you propose?"

Wisdom could tell Satan struggled not to appear too eager.

"Take your protection away—take away your blessing and let me torture him, and I will show you what manner of man worships you. He will curse you, hate you, and ultimately leave you."

"Very well."

Wisdom's fists clenched. *I will trust the Maker...I will trust the Maker... no matter what happens, I trust Him.*

Elation illuminated Satan's face as he turned to scurry away.

"Oh, and Satan?"

He cringed, peeking over his shoulder.

"You may not touch his person. Remember that."

A scowl darkened Satan's face, but he nodded and fled.

The throne room remained silent.

"Maker?" Wisdom whispered. "You practically shoved Job at Satan."

"Watch, dearest, and see what manner of man worships me."

Wisdom turned toward the brightly colored orb with a sinking heart. She knew all about man's heart and the wickedness within— even those who loved her Creator as much as she did.

      ✤ ✤ ✤

Wisdom's heart ached with each tragedy that befell Job. Was the Maker finished letting Satan touch His beloved? She trudged into the council room, later than normal with her report.

Her back stiffened when she saw who stood before the King. Again.

"Satan. Where do you come from?" the King was asking.

Satan looked annoyed. "From roaming that blasted planet of yours. There's nothing else to do."

The Master smirked. "And what think you of My servant Job? He withstood your test very nicely, don't you think? He did not once sin in anything he did or said."

Satan snorted. "Of course he didn't curse you! A man will give anything he has to save his own life. I bet if you struck his body with pain and disease he would curse you to your face."

The King nodded. "He is in your hand. Only spare his life."

Glee erupted on Satan's face, and he bolted from the chamber. "Maker, really?"

The King's eyes settled on Wisdom.

"You have something you wish to say, Wisdom?"

All eyes swiveled to the Creator's master craftsman. Wisdom swallowed and stepped forward.

"Maker, please help me understand. What good will this accomplish? Why test Job so? Forgive me, You know I trust You, but this seems so very cruel. Why let Satan torment someone who loves You so wholeheartedly? There are so very few who do so as it is."

The Maker walked toward her. His eyes never left hers. He gathered her hands in His own.

"Wisdom, watch carefully. You will see how My glory is revealed. Man's suffering is but for a little while, but My power and might are for eternity. With Me, Job can do this."

❈ ❈ ❈

"Folly, you are a genius!"

Folly gasped as Lucifer's arms came around her. She flinched, but he hefted her in his arms and spun her in a circle. Her head reeled after he released her. What had he just said? Genius. Her?

He gripped her shoulders tightly. "Not only did the master give me permission, he's letting me do far more than I ever dreamed possible!"

A grin flared to life on Folly's face. She laughed, thrilled something she had suggested had gone right.

"Why, that's wonderful, Lucifer."

126

"I've destroyed everything the maker gave him, and just came from giving the man boils." He grinned. "I've never seen so many oozing sores on one of those creatures before. It is delicious."

Folly's grin slipped. She wanted to be happy about that, she really did, but the maker had somehow cursed her with his compassion. Ever since she had met the master before pushing Lamech to murder, sorrow welled within her every time something awful happened to the maker's creatures. Even if she did that awful thing herself.

"Oh. That's...wonderful."

Lucifer's tolerant look let her know she sounded as inane as she thought she sounded. Great.

"Don't get too excited there, Folly."

Folly winced. She didn't dare explain whatever curse the maker had put on her. The last thing she wanted to do was empathize with the creatures. Or let Lucifer know she did.

"I have a job for you."

"Oh?"

"Yes." He looked her over carefully. "You are one of my better-looking angels. I need you to go to Job's friends. I've picked three of his closest companions. Once you tell them my message, suggest they visit and comfort their friend in his suffering."

Folly nodded. "With pleasure." She turned to leave.

"Um, one more thing."

She paused, fear trickling into her heart. Did she want to know? She peeked back at him.

"I want you to disguise yourself as a heavenly angel. An angel of light."

Folly blinked. That was brilliant. A grin worked its way onto her face.

"Absolutely."

She hurried from the room.

This was going to be amazing.

❋ ❋ ❋

Wisdom pulled back from watching her sister talk with Satan.

She needed to speak to Elihu. Immediately.

❀ ❀ ❀

Folly knew the moment Eliphaz felt her presence. Still in deep sleep, a tremble coursed through his body. Then another. Fear seeped out of him. She stepped into his dream.

He stood in an empty, dark space, his eyes wild, frantic. He searched for her.

She grinned. Time to have some fun.

Breezing past him, Folly stayed just out of sight. Her image blurred before him, but his sharp intake of breath was enough. She had his attention.

She stepped in front of him and stood still. Her shimmering white dress had the desired effect. He relaxed, but she could tell he was still afraid. She kept her image hazy so he couldn't quite see her, and she hoped her black wings blended with the darkness enough so he wouldn't see them and become even more alarmed. Some fear was good. Not too much. Not this time.

His entire being shook, but he didn't take his eyes off of her. She glanced at his arms. The hairs stood on end. Perfect.

Folly waited, letting him get used to her. Gauging whether he would shut her out or listen to her voice. The silence was deep, full of meaning.

She dropped her voice to a whisper.

"Can a mere mortal please his god? Can a human be purer than his maker? Can he even attempt to be righteous? If the lord does not trust his servants, and he reprimands his angels and tells them they did wrong, how much more those who are made from dust? They are broken, they perish, and no one even cares! Doesn't their beauty and intelligence depart as they age? They die, alone and without Wisdom. What chance does Job have?"

She smiled. Truth mixed with lies. Mostly lies, actually. Just enough truth to sound right.

He didn't even hesitate. He bowed before her, speechless.

"Go quickly. Speak with Bildad and Zophar. Take them to comfort

128

Job. You have heard the word of the lord."

His agreement was unspoken but clear.

Folly grinned. Off to see the other two now. Bildad and Zophar.

❊ ❊ ❊

The Creator's face darkened with each lengthy tangent between Job and his three friends. Wisdom could feel His scowl. True, Job had not sinned in anything he had said…until this point. Now Job demanded the Master answer to him for all the wrong that had happened. Instead of trusting in His Creator and asking for deliverance, Job accepted everything Satan threw at him, then wallowed in self-pity. Then when his friends antagonized him, Job said he had done nothing wrong and insisted the Almighty explain Himself.

The Maker shifted in His throne and rubbed His jaw. He may have known exactly what was going to happen, but that didn't make it any less painful to watch —for Him or for Wisdom. The King shook His head after one particularly irksome statement from Eliphaz.

Wisdom quite agreed. She wanted to strangle the "friends" who had supposedly come to comfort Job. They had done nothing but discourage him further. Now they sat in a circle and argued, each raising his voice louder than the last. Finally —*finally*—a strained silence ensued. The four friends crossed their arms and refused to look at each other.

She glanced at Elihu. Would he say anything? Eliphaz, Bildad, and Zophar had agreed he could accompany them, only if he didn't speak. They didn't want him to make Job feel worse. Yeah. That had worked well for them.

The King pointed to Wisdom, then Elihu. Elihu was seething nearly as much as she had been. Wisdom nodded, then flew down and landed next to Elihu. Strife hissed at her. She silenced the fallen angel with a sharp glance, then nudged Elihu with her foot.

He startled at her touch, and his mouth snapped open.

"Really, Job? Really? You justify yourself rather than God? I have sat here, in silence, in respect, confident that the years of all of your knowledge would speak the obvious. Certain that each of you would listen to Wisdom. Who am I? A youth. The least among you. Yet you bicker and argue and let Folly take hold of each of your hearts. How mighty is our God? How vast is His knowledge? And yet, *you* are righteous, and He is not?"

Wisdom hurried back to the Creator's side.

The Maker stood and joined her, arms crossed.

Finally!

Wisdom grinned. She loved to see this side of Him.

Elihu kept talking, and Wisdom's heart warmed. He had listened well to her. She watched Job's face carefully. He wasn't listening. She glanced at his friends. Neither were they. What on earth?

Wisdom stepped forward. The Maker's hand grasped her elbow.

"I've got this."

The King stepped down to the planet below, breaching the height, width, and depth with one step.

A vortex swirled around Him, blocking the mortals' view of their Creator.

The fallen angels enjoying the argument fled.

"Which of you darkens counsel with words filled with ignorance? Prepare yourself, Job. Act like a man, and answer Me this. Where were you when I laid the foundations of the earth?"

Job and his friends listened in rapt attention as the Maker matched their long-winded discussion with His own discourse. Only this one was filled with truth. Elihu prostrated himself before the booming voice.

"Will you strive against the Almighty, then correct Him? Answer Me, Job. Are you rebuking God?"

Job clasped his hand over his mouth as tears filled his eyes. He shook his head.

"I have sinned once already with my mouth. I won't do it again, Lord."

The Maker wasn't finished.

"Prepare yourself, Job. Act like a man, and answer me this. Will you really count My judgment as nothing? Do you condemn Me, yet justify yourself?"

Job threw himself before the whirlwind.

"I now know You can do anything You want, O King. I didn't understand what I was saying. You don't answer to me or anyone else. Now that I see You, I despise myself and repent for every word I uttered. Forgive me, my Master."

The King waited, but the three friends sat dumb, not one speaking. Or looking very sorry for what they had said. Wisdom shook her head. They truly thought they had heard from angels. The Maker's angels. What would Satan try next?

The Maker spoke to Eliphaz.

"Since you and your friends have spoken lies and have listened to Folly instead of Wisdom, offer sacrifices and have Job pray for you. Only then will I forgive you. I will answer Job's prayers, not yours, because you spoke foolish words instead of what was right, like Job did."

"I will—we will."

The tornado vanished, and with it, the King. Wisdom watched Elihu stare after the vortex with longing.

The Maker walked past Wisdom.

"Well that was painful," Wisdom muttered.

"Tell me about it," He agreed. The King snapped His fingers. A messenger stepped forward. "Go to Satan. Tell him I wish to speak with him."

The angel bowed, then flew toward earth.

"Wisdom, come with Me."

Wisdom fell into step beside the Maker. He sat on His throne, and Wisdom stood beside Him. They didn't have to wait long.

Satan, skittish, eyes darting everywhere, stepped forward. "Yes, your majesty?"

The King leaned back in His throne, relaxed.

"What do you think of My servant, Job?"

Satan winced. "He performed...remarkably."

He choked on the final word.

"And are you satisfied?"

Satan's face turned a mottled red. After a visible struggle, he nodded.

"Quite."

The King leaned forward.

"Remember My words to you in the garden, father of lies. Your defeat is certain."

Hatred sparked from Satan's eyes. A vein throbbed on his forehead. The King continued.

"You may not touch one of My creatures who trust in Me without My permission."

Satan growled low in his throat. "I know."

"Do you? Make sure of it. They are Mine. And when they learn their authority comes from Me, you will have to listen to *them*."

"Oh, really."

Satan shoved his hands on his hips and started to argue.

"Really. Out."

Satan snapped his mouth closed and turned to leave, fists clenched.

"And I expect a full report of your activities when My princes come to give their reports."

Satan didn't turn but inclined his head to the side. Wisdom waited until he was back on the planet to speak.

"Maker, why?"

"I want him to never forget he answers to Me."

"But why would you give him permission to test your saints?"

The King offered her a small smile. "Only through battle will they learn how to defeat their enemy. Don't worry, Wisdom. They will overcome if they trust Me. And their faith will be strengthened if they persevere."

The Master stood and walked toward His chambers.

"Maker?"

He stopped. "Yes, Wisdom?"

"What of Job now?"

He smiled. "Go to his friends, his family—all who know him. Tell them to comfort him and to each give him a silver coin and a gold ring. I aim to bless him with more than he ever had before. Oh, yes. And plan something especially delightful for Elihu."

Wisdom returned His smile. "It will be my pleasure."

She sprinted for earth, eager to carry out the Creator's wishes. Job deserved every good thing the King had in store for him. And she would make sure Satan never touched Job again.

Chapter Fourteen

Wisdom has built her house, she has hewn out her seven pillars; she has slaughtered her meat, she has mixed her wine, she has also furnished her table. She has sent out her maidens, she cries from the highest places of the city, "Whoever is simple, let him turn in here!"
Proverbs 9:1-4

Wisdom ran the plane down the length of the wood, her fingers trailing the smooth surface as another shaving curled to the ground. Hefting the finished pillar in her hands, she carefully dropped it into its hole. The weight of it sank deep and held fast. She stepped back and gazed at her work.

"It's beautiful."

Wisdom yelped and spun around. Wrapping her sister in a stranglehold, she jumped up and down.

"Discretion! What are you doing here? I thought you said once was enough!"

"I missed you." Discretion smiled, then a greenish hue overtook her face. "I may stay for a while, though."

Wisdom laughed joyously. "Of course, stay as long as you like! What do you think? Want to help me finish the roof?"

Discretion paled. "No, thank you. I'll stay right here with my feet firmly planted on planet terra." Her gaze roved over the house Wisdom was building. "It is lovely. Where ever did you get the idea?"

Wisdom grinned. "Inspired by the Maker, of course. The seven pillars represent the seven spirits who worship at His throne day and night. The pearled doors resemble the gates of heaven, and the many chambers are for those who wish to learn here, just like the many chambers the Lord had me craft in heaven. Just a small taste of what awaits them. I'm so excited the Master is letting me do this; I can hardly wait!"

Discretion smiled bemusedly. "Yes, dear, I can see that. Do you think anyone will come?"

"Well…" Wisdom busied herself with stacking shingles. She was amazed at how much the truthful words stung. She had been trying *not* to think them for days. She sighed and looked at her masterpiece. "I certainly hope so."

"Me too, dear. Me too."

They gazed in silence a few moments longer, then a worried frown creased Discretion's forehead.

"Where on earth is your water?"

Wisdom groaned. "I should have known that was coming." She pointed. "Out back." Wisdom grabbed her sister's arm as she moved away. "It stays out back. In case my guests want to refresh themselves or rest under the trees."

"Nonsense, love. Not all of it. Your new house will need a reflecting pool or two, and you know how soothing the Lord's creatures find the sound of tinkling waterfalls. Don't worry. I'll only put in a few."

Wisdom groaned as Discretion moved away.

"Why don't I just build your room in the middle of the lake?" she called after her sister.

A surprised grin lit Discretion's face as she glanced back at Wisdom.

"You would do that?"

"Yes. Yes, I would. Just…please…go easy on the amount of water in my home."

"Deal."

Discretion hurried away, off to investigate the most important part of Wisdom's newest dwelling. To her, anyway.

Wisdom shook her head and began shaping the next pillar.

Man, but it was good to see her sister again.

❖ ❖ ❖

Wisdom distributed the hand-crafted invitations with care.

"Each of these will go to the kings, princes, and advisors of terra."

As she handed a parchment copy to her maidens, the original glass-inscribed invitation stayed in her grasp. Ella, one of the smaller messengers, kept looking behind Wisdom. Ella's gaze kept drifting to the newly constructed, sprawling mansion Wisdom had built.

"Pay attention, Ella."

Ella's head whipped around. Her face flushed.

"Sorry, Wisdom."

Wisdom gave the angel a gentle smile. She turned back to the curled parchment she pulled from her glass copy. She handed it to the next maiden.

"Now, you will speak with decorum and respect, and invite all who wish to learn from me to do so. Read the invitation word for word."

She lifted the crystal sheet and read aloud.

To the kings and princes and advisors of the earth:

Those who would be wise, learn from me!

Come, eat at my table and drink my wine.

Forsake your foolish ways and seek life—seek understanding.

Fear the Lord, for only then will you understand true wisdom.

Know the Holy One, and He will teach you all things.

Only by me are your days multiplied,

And years added to your life.

Come, learn from me, and enjoy abundant life!

Penned by the hand of Lady Wisdom

She dropped the sheet to her side.

"Questions?"

Ella's hand shot up.

"Yes, Ella."

She bounced with excitement. "Before we go, may we look at your house, please?"

If she would have clasped her hands under her chin and tilted her head, she couldn't have looked any more like a little child pleading for something she desperately wanted. Wisdom tried to stifle her grin, to look commanding, in charge. Didn't work. She laughed.

"Yes, Ella. You may all have a tour before you leave. But please, hurry. I want these halls filled past bursting with students."

The girls laughed and chatted, streaming behind Wisdom as she led them toward her house of learning.

Wisdom sighed.

Lord, you are so good! Thank you for letting me teach your precious creatures face-to-face. I can hardly wait!

His love wrapped around her and overwhelmed her.

I love you so, dearest Wisdom. You are most welcome.

Wisdom reveled in the embrace until she realized…a slight warning touched her soul like a hint of vapor.

She stopped, her maidens walking past her.

There wouldn't be many students.

Her jaw tightened. She marched toward her home.

There would be if she had anything to do with it.

A feather-soft touch brushed her cheek, fading into nothing.

"Please, Maker," she whispered.

❊ ❊ ❊

Amber stood before a king.

"Wisdom herself, huh?"

Amber tilted her head in affirmation.

The king let the roll snap back into a curl.

"Sounds perfect! I'll just have the servants get my things together and be there in say, six or seven months?"

A servant hustled forward and whispered in the king's ear.

"Oh. Yes. Well, after a few meetings and a visit from the king of the Orient. Then I'll come."

Amber bowed slightly. "If you please, your majesty, I can take you now if you but come with me."

The king laughed. "What of my servants? And the caravan? Travel to your Wisdom's palace will take quite some time, you know."

137

A hint of a smile graced Amber's face. "It can take much less if you allow me to make travel arrangements. Also, the Lady Wisdom has her own servants to attend to your needs. You'll want for nothing under her roof."

The emotions on the king's face wavered between uncertainty and acceptance. Amber pressed forward, voice calm.

"An invitation from Wisdom is a very precious and coveted thing, your majesty. I would not keep her waiting."

The king nodded. "Very well. Let me attend to my responsibilities. Then I will join you and your Wisdom."

Amber's face clouded, but she bowed in respect.

"As you wish, your majesty."

She turned and left his hall. Amber knew his cares would keep him from attending Wisdom's school. She vanished from sight once she was alone and unfurled her wings. Wisdom needed to know. She would be disappointed, but Amber had every intention of asking the king again and again—as many times as it took.

✿ ✿ ✿

Wisdom listened to Amber's report with a sinking heart. It was the same thing she had heard over and over again in the past few weeks.

Only three out of hundreds had accepted her invitation.

Amber fell silent. Wisdom dropped her head.

Amber's soft voice lilted with certainty. "I will ask him again, Wisdom."

Wisdom laughed and shook her head. "How can they not want to come?" Glancing up at Amber, she straightened. "No. If the kings and princes and wise men do not wish to attend my school, I shall send for the others. Place *them* in positions of authority. Amber, call the other girls. I have a new invitation to write."

Head bent over her desk, Wisdom didn't hear Amber leave as she scratched out new invitations.

✿ ✿ ✿

Jasmine stood in a hovel, an angry woman clutching a clay pot under white knuckles.

"I don't take kindly to pranks, young lady. Not when it comes to my son."

"My lady, please. This is no prank." Jasmine bent and retrieved the torn scroll from the dirt-encrusted floor. She held the two halves together, then thought better of repairing it in front of the woman and her son. "Wisdom has indeed invited Hakeem to study under her."

The woman's glower turned even more fierce.

"And why would she pay my son any mind?"

Jasmine fought off a sigh. *Patience, Lord. Grant me lots and lots of patience.*

It's yours, came His swift reply.

Thank you, Almighty King.

She tried to explain it to the woman. Again.

"Your son will need her guidance one day. He…"

"Why?"

"I can't say, my lady. Only that he will need to be prepared. Wisdom offers him long life and blessings if he will but learn from her."

The mother jerked her head toward her son, who was standing behind her. Jasmine glanced at the lad. His expression was pained, embarrassed, and fighting to control his mounting excitement. Jasmine's pulse quickened. He was listening, at least.

"Can't say my boy is interested."

"With all due respect, my lady, the invitation is for him alone. It is his choice to refuse or accept it." She turned her gaze to him. "What do you say, Hakeem? Will you accept Lady Wisdom's invitation? Will you learn from her?"

His mother sputtered, but Hakeem placed a hand on her shoulder. He squeezed and stepped around her.

"I gladly accept the invitation, and I thank you."

Jasmine nodded. "Come then."

"May I gather my things?"

Jasmine smiled. "All your needs will be provided for. Come and taste and see that the Lord is good."

A grunt sounded from behind him.

"I think there is wisdom in knowing your place—your station in life. Not trying to be better than what you are."

Jasmine lifted a brow. "There is also prudence in allowing Wisdom to exalt one she has called. Please, don't let your parting be in strife." She glanced between the two. "I shall wait for you outside, Hakeem."

Although she stood outside of the dwelling, offering protection against thieves and murderers, she could still hear their voices.

"I do not like it. You are a nothing. A nobody. No good like your father before you."

Jasmine's fists clenched. Hakeem released a heavy sigh.

"I know you do not believe me, but I don't want to be like him. I long for more. To make a better life for us. For me. Please. I have prayed for this with every fiber in my being."

His mother sniffed.

"Fine. Go. But do not come back."

A door slammed.

Jasmine entered and waited for Hakeem to lift his head before uncloaking herself. His eyes widened in surprise.

"Are you ready?"

He straightened, pulling his shoulders back.

"I am."

Invisible wings stretched behind her. She stepped forward and wrapped them tightly around him, and, in an instant, he stood before Wisdom's house. Hakeem blinked, then staggered when she released him. Jasmine smiled. Knowing he was unaware of how he had arrived, Jasmine tugged on his hand.

"Come. I will introduce you to Wisdom."

Chapter Fifteen

For He satisfies the longing soul, and fills the hungry soul with goodness.
Psalm 107:9

"Goodbye, Hakeem. Safe journeys, and may God speed you on your way."

Hakeem nodded and dropped his head. Emotion clogged his throat, and his voice came out deep and husky.

"I will never forget you, Wisdom. Thank you for all you have taught me. Thank you — for taking me in."

A sheen of moisture coated Wisdom's eyes. She cleared her throat and nodded.

"And I, you. You are most welcome."

Hakeem bowed, and, tugging on his Arabian's bridle, led the horse away.

Wisdom watched him mount at the bottom of the hill, soon disappearing down the trail curving out of sight.

She sighed and propped her hands on her hips. Almost a thousand years, and still only a handful of creatures had come to learn from her. Hakeem — her most recent student — had stayed the longest, his thirst for wisdom and knowledge nearly unquenchable.

She watched Hakeem through the thick forest. He would make a cunning and conscientious wise man. She prayed he would follow the Creator in his homeland — she prayed he would pass down what he had learned to future generations.

"Another student passes your testing."

Wisdom offered Discretion a wobbly smile.

"Yes," she sighed. "I will miss him."

"You miss each of your creatures when they leave you. Tell me; do you like this better? Them coming to you, I mean."

Wisdom shrugged, telling herself to snap out of it—she could see Hakeem anytime. Even if he couldn't see her outside of this magical place, she could still check on him.

"Out there"—she nodded past the thick wood—"I can whisper into their hearts, and they can choose whether to listen or not. Here…" She gazed around her beloved home before meeting Discretion's eyes. "Here I can fellowship with them, and they *want* to learn from me. They don't simply dismiss my words because it doesn't follow what they want to do. They listen, learn—become truly wise, filled with understanding. These wise men and women take their knowledge back to their kingdoms, become advisors, ladies-in-waiting, wives to powerful men; they influence the world."

Wisdom yearned to make Discretion understand. Discretion hadn't seen much fruit from Wisdom's endeavors and was ever skeptical.

"What of the kings and princes? I haven't seen many of those."

Wisdom shook her head, her shoulders drooping.

"No. Not many wish to learn from the Lord."

"And the Hebrews?"

Wisdom bit back a laugh. Discretion just never gave up, did she?

"Someday. For now, I will keep going to them. The Lord's chosen people. I wish they listened to me, especially."

"David listens to you."

Wisdom shrugged and smiled as she thought of the zealous king with enough passion to rival her own. If only all creatures sought the Maker as David did!

"Mostly. I am glad for that."

"What about him? Have you had one of your servants ask him to come here?"

"Of course. But he is busy. Always too busy, even when he was hiding from Saul."

"Seems like the perfect time to have joined you," Discretion intoned drily.

Wisdom nodded and continued. "Most kings and princes are too busy with their earthly kingdoms to learn from me here, even if they should..." Wisdom speared her sister with a desperate stare. "Why won't they listen to me, Discretion? Why do they choose their own way, instead of the Maker's best for them? It goes so much better for them when they follow Him and do what He says. What am I doing wrong? Why aren't my halls filled past bursting? Why aren't my libraries overflowing with seekers of truth? Why, Discretion? Why?"

Discretion wrapped her in a gentle hug.

"Because they are fallen, dearest. We must show mercy and lead them to Him, whether they listen or not. And don't forget those who do listen; they are making a difference. Keep calling to them, keep guiding them, keep doing what you are doing, sister. The Maker sees and hears. He knows of your desperate love for His creation. Your efforts will not be in vain, I promise."

Wisdom chuckled, loving her sister's clarity when everything seemed so very clouded.

"Want to teach my next class, Discretion?"

"No, thanks. I can think of nothing less appealing than spending hours pouring over a subject that the creatures can only grasp the most rudimentary concepts. It makes me want to tear my hair out every time I hear you agonizing over the most basic teachings."

Wisdom shook her head. "Worse than flying, you mean?"

Discretion's face paled. "Nothing is worse than that. On second thought, maybe I'll teach that class."

Wisdom laughed outright. Movement caught her attention.

"Oh, look. You've got your wish. Your very first student, sister."

Discretion blanched even further. "I, uh, I'll just see about fixing that stream that runs through the property. It needs to be moved a bit to the west for the, uh, fish."

Discretion bustled away as Wisdom laughed.

Wisdom watched her sister fly down the heavily wooded path, away from Wisdom's new guests.

Discretion's stay had lasted much longer than Wisdom thought it would, and she was grateful. Having her sister at her home made everything seem—lighter. Easier. Her burden didn't feel so heavy.

Being the primary angel who led the creatures away from destruction, tugging them toward life, weighed heavily on her. If they didn't listen to her, they didn't live well. Or very long.

She turned her gaze to the threesome picking their way toward her through the foliage.

One of Wisdom's maidens led a woman and a small boy to her house.

Wisdom waited to speak until they paused not far from the house. The woman and boy stared at it past her, while Wisdom's servant waited for them to be able to see Wisdom.

Wisdom dismissed her servant with a nod. The angel glided past her, a satchel in each hand.

"Welcome."

The woman tore her gaze away and glanced around the clearing. She bowed once she caught sight of Wisdom's face.

The woman was beautiful. Exceedingly so. Honey brown hair curled from beneath her head covering. The subdued clothing did not hide her tall, womanly frame. Light brown-hued eyes and a lightly tanned face turned upward to meet Wisdom's gaze.

"I have brought my son to enroll in your school. Are you—?"

The woman tilted her head and paused.

"Wisdom."

"Yes. Wisdom. Are you accepting students?"

Wisdom wanted to laugh, an empty, hollow sound, but did not. Even if she had no room, she'd take him. She'd build as many rooms as necessary if only her halls were overflowing with lovers of wisdom.

"I am."

"Good."

The woman looked around her uncertainly. She held out a small bundle.

"His clothes."

Wisdom gently took it from her, careful their hands didn't touch.

"All right then. I should be back to get him…I'm not sure when…" She bit her lip, her eyes flitting away.

"Be at peace, your majesty."

She stared at Wisdom, eyes wide.

"How did you know?" she managed in a strangled whisper.

"Do not fear, Bathsheba. The Maker reveals to me what I need to know, nothing more. Your son will be safe here, and you will be able to return for him in a year's time. I will teach him well."

The air whooshed out of Bathsheba's willowy frame.

"Praise Yahweh."

Crouching down, she turned her son to face her.

"Solomon, I have to go away for a little while, but I will come back for you. I promise. Be good for Wisdom, and I want to hear all about your time here when I return, understand?"

The boy nodded solemnly.

She tugged him close and whispered in his ear.

"I love you more than the stars in the heavens."

She turned and fled down the hillside.

Solomon watched her, his face hidden from Wisdom. But she could feel his emotions course over her.

Fear. Abandonment. Confusion. Deep, deep sadness.

He turned and looked at her, long after his mother had disappeared from sight. His large, mournful eyes—the same shade as his mother's—stared at her without flinching. A crusted gash ran from his temple to his jaw. His eye was purpled and swollen.

Wisdom reached out and tousled his hair. The dark brown strands curled around her fingers and sprang back into place.

His expression didn't change.

She ran her finger down the length of the wound. The skin knit together and evened out. The purple faded, and the swelling dimmed to nothing.

He didn't flinch.

She held out her hand. "Come, dearest one. I'll show you where you will be staying. Tomorrow, lessons begin."

He didn't acknowledge he had heard her, just followed her. Walking tall. Standing straight. Emotionless face. The tight pressure of his hand the only outward sign of his inner struggle.

She led him down the corridor, pausing outside an ornate, wooden door.

"Wait here, please."

She gently closed the door behind her. Her servant gave her a swift smile as she fluffed the mattress and curled sheets and blankets around it. Wisdom nodded at her. Lifting her fingers, the room shifted. It now resembled the room he shared with his mother in the palace's harem.

Enough to help him feel at home, but not too much. Too much and he would feel even more lost.

She stood back and the door swung open soundlessly. The maiden vanished. Solomon stood without, no change in expression. He hadn't moved. She waited, an encouraging smile beckoning him forward. He entered, head tall. Yet she could feel him drooping inside.

Wisdom waved her hand and clouds darkened the streaming sunlight.

"Rest, dearest. You will feel better in the morning."

He crawled into the bed without complaint. She tucked him in, resting her fingers on his forehead. His eyes drifted shut. A slight breeze lifted the gauzy curtains, and Wisdom checked to make sure the temperature was to his liking. The room fell by a few more degrees.

Only five years old. And already growing up before his time.

She stepped into the shadow by the door and glanced behind her. The little eyes were wide open and staring at the ceiling. She quickly cloaked herself from sight. He peeked to make sure she was gone. Sobs heaved out of the little body, and he fisted his hands over his eyes, struggling to keep his weeping quiet.

On silent feet, Wisdom moved back to his side. She curled up on the bed next to him, and he snuggled into her without knowing she held him. She sang to him and stroked his wild curls while he cried himself to sleep.

❈ ❈ ❈

"What happened?"

Wisdom tossed the basket of bread, cheese, and wine too roughly on the wrap-around counter in the middle of her kitchen. It tipped and an apple rolled onto the floor.

Discretion wordlessly uprighted the skin of wine, pulled out a jar of goat's milk, and rummaged through several pieces of fruit. She glanced at Wisdom.

"Our orchards aren't good enough all of a sudden?"

Wisdom waved her hand dismissively.

"I got him a few of his favorite foods while I was at the palace. I thought it might make him feel better."

Discretion grinned at her.

"Taken with the little guy, are we? All right, spill it. I can see you don't want to tell me. Best to get it all out in the open."

Wisdom sighed and rubbed her face.

"David is away at battle and will be for some time. His other wives are, of course, jealous over David's new favorite wife."

Discretion nodded.

Wisdom slammed her fist against the table.

"I mean, what was he thinking? The Maker clearly instructs Israel's kings to take only one wife, not to amass horses, to rely on the *Lord* for their riches, and not to tax the people out of everything they own. How can he expect not to have trouble when he disregards everything the Master says?"

"Careful, sister. You are speaking against the Creator's beloved. He loves David fiercely. Besides, you said yourself he does listen to you."

Wisdom dropped her head, red staining her cheeks.

"Forgive me, sister. I spoke out of turn."

"You spoke truth. But remember it is not our place to speak against the Master's creatures. Now, why is Solomon here, without his father's knowledge?"

Wisdom bowed her head, beseeching the Maker for forgiveness for her angry words.

Forgiveness came swiftly. Wisdom felt a brief hug. The feeling faded as fast as it came. It had been too long since she had basked in His presence, doing nothing else. She couldn't even remember the last time she had taken Him a report. She would remedy that. A prolonged visit to the Maker was just what she needed. Right after she helped Solomon.

Wisdom took a shaky breath, determined to speak words of life, not frustration.

"David is away at battle, and one of the older sons took it upon himself to kill David's favorite son. Praise the Maker he didn't succeed! Bathsheba has hidden him away until David can return and offer the boy his protection."

Wisdom shivered, rubbing at her arms. The creature's cruelty to one another amazed her. Did they care nothing for the lifeblood from the Maker flowing through their veins?

Discretion frowned. "Will the boy be safe, even after his father's return? David doesn't spend much time at the harem. His protection would be minimal."

"I will see to it the boy is protected!"

Wisdom's fierce voice rose and fell away, its echo a promise.

"I don't doubt it. Until then, you will teach him? You don't think he's too young to remember?"

"The younger, the better, Discretion. Then it is hidden in his heart and will direct his path. He may not remember me or my lessons specifically, but he will always remember my concepts. Deep down. He will make the right choices. He will."

Discretion glanced out the window. Planting a tender kiss on her sister's forehead, she slipped out of the room.

Wisdom stared at the wall, fists clenched, heart furious that such evil was in the world.

"Folly," Wisdom growled.

"Oh, you heard me?"

Folly slipped inside from the shadows without. She slinked against the farthest wall, eyes darting around the room. Her posture spoke of unease and flippancy at once. She grinned at Wisdom.

Wisdom grimaced. Folly's sneer was lopsided—cruel to the very core. Her skin was mottled, scarred, and pulled tight against one side of her mouth.

"Imagine my surprise when the house I couldn't get within a hundred yards of suddenly opened to me. Quite an…interesting… place you've built, sister."

Folly's gaze traveled the room again, her smirk holding derision. Behind her smirk, behind her mockery, Wisdom detected something else. What was it? What was her sister hiding?

"And it will be closed to you the instant we are through."

Folly raised a warped brow against too-pale skin, her flint-gray eyes empty of life.

"Not afraid to let me near your precious student?"

"You cannot harm him here, nor can he see you or feel your presence."

Folly shrugged and picked at her bleeding fingertips, looking bored.

Wisdom's voice shattered the prolonged silence.

"Why?"

Folly's eyes snagged on Wisdom and held.

"Why, what?"

"Why would you try to kill a child? How could you?"

Folly smirked, crossing her arms and leaning against the wall.

"Wasn't me. Was that boy—what's-his-name. Jealous as all of David's wives put together."

Wisdom shook with anger.

"You stay away from him, you hear me? He is under my protection now. Try anything like that again and I will personally see to it the Maker never lets you out of that hell-hole again, do you understand me?"

Folly blanched.

"You wouldn't. I mean, you couldn't."

"Try me."

The sisters stared at each other, neither one breaking away from the other's gaze.

"Fine. I won't harm him again." Folly raised her chin defiantly.

"Get out."

"With pleasure."

Folly's eyes pinged around the room once more before she vanished, reappearing far away. Wisdom instantly raised the veiled protection around the cove of learning.

Folly's last glance hit Wisdom like a blow.

Wisdom sat back, amazed.

"She misses it," she whispered.

"Do you think she'll listen?"

Wisdom glanced at Discretion, wondering how much she had overheard.

"I've never seen such fear on our sister's face. She'll listen."

"Do you think the Maker would really confine her?"

Wisdom's jaw clenched.

"I would see to it that He did."

❊ ❊ ❊

Folly closed her eyes and listened to the sound of the sea lapping against the stony shore.

She took several deep breaths to still the tremors that shook her.

The nerve of Wisdom to tell her what she could and couldn't do! That she would be confined to that rotting prison, never again to breathe the maker-laden air!

Jumping to her feet, Folly paced the rim of the cliff jutting out to nothing, water far below.

She clenched her fists, trying to still their quaking, trying to draw the anger—her ever-present companion—from deep within her. It wouldn't come.

She plopped back on the rock, dejected.

I miss her so much!

Folly blinked away tears, refusing to cry.

Her mind replayed her visit, over and over.

Wisdom looked well. Older—perhaps wiser, more steady, if that were even possible. Gravity clung to her where gaiety and eagerness had been before. Desperation and fierce protection lit her eyes as she spoke of the boy.

Folly cocked her head.

Wisdom's self-imposed perfection, her desperate need to make sure everything she did for the master was flawless, was her greatest strength.

I wonder how I can use that against her?

A niggling idea formed in Folly's mind even as despair crashed over her. She couldn't even plot against her sister with this blasted longing inside of her! She pushed thoughts of ensnaring Wisdom away. She would think about that later. After she had taken care of Solomon.

One thing was certain, her sister had grown more beautiful with the slow march of time. More beautiful than even Folly remembered.

Folly stared down at her scarred arms.

What had Wisdom seen when she looked at her?

She leaned far over the edge, trying to catch a glimpse of herself in the turbulent waters. The waves crashed and churned, refusing her one, simple request to see what her sister saw.

"Fine," she snarled. "Keep your mirror to yourself. I didn't want to see anyway."

The sea crashed high with a roar, but even the tiny droplets of spray refused to touch her.

The water had been as tortured to touch her during the deluge as she had been to drown in it.

Folly's head snapped up as an idea pummeled her mind.

She dropped back down on the rock, heart plunging.

Oh, no. Anything but that. Anything.

Praise to the maker still whispered from each water droplet, but Folly didn't hear.

She might not be able to touch the boy, Solomon, but she knew someone who could.

Chapter Sixteen

The wicked plots against the just, and gnashes at him with his teeth. The Lord laughs at him, for He sees that his day is coming.
Psalm 37:12-13

Folly paced.

Back and forth. Back and forth.

"Where is she?" Folly snarled to the darkness.

"Waiting for someone?"

Folly spun around, instantly feeling foolish and gawkish. Why couldn't she, for once, feel at ease around Lust, and not like a child growing her adult legs and arms?

"What took you so long?" Folly hissed.

Lust's eyes snapped with fire.

"I don't answer to you."

Lust spun to leave.

Folly growled and rolled her eyes, hating herself.

"Wait! I — I need to talk to you."

Lust paused, tilting her head, but she didn't turn around.

"I need to ask you something."

Lust stood very still.

Folly sighed. "A favor."

Lust turned slowly, a beaming smile on her face.

"Well, well, well. At last. Come to the expert on something you couldn't handle? What is it, dear? Need help seducing someone? I have a few tricks, you know."

Folly flushed and looked away. Lust's methods were downright humiliating. Folly stayed far away from the prostitutes and temples of the sex goddesses, preferring murder and deceit and rage to the more…baser…of sins.

"No, not exactly—well, yes. And, I can help you get back into Lucifer's good graces."

Lust stood close, her face lit with eager anticipation.

"Really? Who is it? Someone I know? Someone I haven't tempted before? Tell me!"

Folly squirmed. She hated sharing. Especially with *her*.

"There is a boy…"

Lust squealed and clapped her hands.

"Oooooo…corrupting a boy! The very best! Get 'em while they're young. What's his name?"

Folly shook Lust's shoulders.

"For heaven's sake, will you calm down and shut up?"

Folly glanced behind her.

Lust nodded and winked conspiratorially.

"I see. A secret. From Lucifer perhaps? Don't worry; your secret's safe with me. Pray, continue."

It'll be a gorgeous day in hell when any secret is safe with you.

"This young boy, he is hidden to us for now."

Lust straightened, looking worried.

"Look, if you need someone to fight, get someone else—"

"Will you hush? I will tell you if you stop blathering on like an idiot!"

Lust's eyes turned stony. Her words, clipped.

"By all means. Continue."

Folly released her and paced, speaking rapidly. Brainstorming.

"This boy, Solomon—you know, David's son?—will soon come out of Wisdom's safety. I need *you* to plant something in him that will be his downfall."

"Wisdom?" Lust interrupted, voice shrill. "You want me to go against Wisdom? No way. Only Lucifer—Death maybe—would risk themselves by angering her. Fear even stays far away."

The bones shuddered in Folly's jaw, she clenched her teeth so hard. Would Wisdom's fame never end? Did the awe of her sister have to follow her *here*, where she had sacrificed everything just to be better than her—just to get *away* from her?

"You won't face her. I promise."

Lust twisted her hands, shifting her weight from one foot to another.

"If you're sure…"

"I am."

Lust could find out on her own of Wisdom's vow to protect the boy. By then she would have already committed herself in front of Lucifer and most everyone else. Lust was shrewd enough to figure out how to get to the boy, once her hand was forced.

"What else?"

"Um, he sees how his mother is treated, the petty fighting in the harem. He's already learning the best ways to appease manipulative and backbiting women. Maybe—I don't know—see to it he is addicted to what you do. Make sure he has a stumbling block before him so large, he can never get around it."

Lust crossed her arms, her gaze narrowed.

"This boy has come to your attention, and foolishness and pettiness are your specialties. Why can't you do it?"

"I just can't, ok?" Folly snapped. "I'm sorry I even asked!"

Folly spun and stomped down the cloistering tunnel, chosen because they were far away from the tunnels Lucifer roamed when he wasn't on earth.

Lust's bark of a laugh grated on Folly's ears.

"Slow down there, princess. Did you hear me say I wouldn't do it? Get your sorry self back here."

Folly paused, clenching her fists.

This is the last time—and I mean the very last time—I do anything she tells me.

She turned and marched back to Lust, chin held high.

"I'll do it, on one condition."

Folly tensed. Why, oh, why, hadn't she thought of that? Lust wouldn't hand out favors without expecting something in return.

"And what is that?" Folly growled through her teeth.

Lust shrugged and glanced around the tiny room, the spark in her eyes belying her complacent expression.

"This Solomon—the king's son? It was my idea. Lucifer or anyone else asks, it was all me. You had nothing to do with it." A grin stretched her mouth wide as she finally stared directly at Folly. "Unless, of course, I mess it up. Then it's all you."

Folly clenched her fists and bit down on her tongue to keep the snarl from escaping her mouth. But she knew she had no choice. Leaving Solomon to Wisdom was not an option.

"Deal."

Lust shot Folly a seductive smile, and Folly's stomach turned.

"It's been a pleasure," she whispered, blowing Folly a kiss.

She disappeared down the narrow hall.

Folly spit where Lust had been standing and wiped her mouth.

"Next time it'll be on you, witch," Folly whispered into the darkness.

※ ※ ※

"Very good, Solomon. Now look at this one."

They stared at the etched glass together.

Solomon spit out the answer before Wisdom could explain the equation to him.

Wisdom's jaw dropped.

"Perfect!"

She left the clear plate floating in the air and grasped his shoulders.

"You didn't see my answers, did you?"

He giggled.

"No."

She shook him playfully and very, very gently.

"Have you been peeking in my scrolls while I ready your lessons?"

He snorted a laugh.

"No."

Wisdom gasped, and shook her finger at him.

"I know! You wrote the equation, didn't you?"

He threw back his head and chortled, the sweet sound perfuming the air.

"No!"

She hugged him tight.

"You are just too smart, Mr. Solomon."

She planted a kiss on his forehead. He jabbed her in the ribs.

"Oh, that's how it's going to be, is it?"

The room pealed with laughter as she tickled him unmercifully.

"Ahem."

Wisdom and Solomon froze, both staring at the doorway.

"Momma!"

Solomon jumped from her arms and bolted into his mother's.

"Oh, how I've missed you! How are you, my darling? Well, I hope?"

Discretion cleared her throat again and nodded several times toward the floating glass.

Wisdom snatched it from the air. It curled into parchment in her fist.

Bathsheba looked at Wisdom, tears in her eyes.

"Thank you," she mouthed.

Wisdom nodded, and Bathsheba led Solomon from the room. His little voice poured from him in waves, telling his mother everything from the second lesson on.

The first lesson was precious to Wisdom and Solomon both. It had been the turning point of his grieving, Solomon seeing her heavenly beauty for the first time. And it was between them like a peace offering, though neither spoke of it.

Discretion moved to her side.

"Sorry, I was having the worst time getting you both to hear me." Discretion smiled. "I think that was good for his mother to see, though. She's been so worried about him."

Wisdom glanced at Discretion in surprise. "She told you?"

Discretion shook her head. "She didn't have to."

Wisdom nodded. "I suppose I should get his things."

Discretion stared long and hard at her.

"How long are you going to do this, sister? It tears you so."

Wisdom stood and left.

She didn't tell Discretion that Solomon would be her last student. Her throat had closed like a vise and she couldn't get the words out if she wanted to. She couldn't bear to see another walk out of those doors to choose his own path instead of the Maker's.

❖ ❖ ❖

Wisdom followed Solomon and his mother into the palace, her school temporarily closed. Her home was hidden from the creature's view—her maidens dispatched to return to the Maker for new orders.

Solomon and his mother would never know how close they had come to not making it back to the palace at all. Bathsheba had made the long trek without servants, fearful of David discovering where she had taken the boy and why. He had returned from battle, triumphant, wanting to visit his wives and children after the sacrifices of thanksgiving. Bathsheba fairly flew to collect Solomon, and Wisdom sped them on their journey, making the miles disappear like the smoke from their campfire. Wisdom had shielded them—and their campfire—from a group of bandits following them, intent on harm.

Wisdom had covered them with her wings, daring the fallen angels accompanying the robbers to provoke her. Hate and Destruction had shied away, dropping their gazes as they let their too-easily-persuaded thieves wander away in their search. Not many of the fallen would dare go against Wisdom, not with the fire of battle in her eyes, and Wisdom knew it.

Now anger surged in Wisdom's heart as she walked the hallways of the harem.

Wives milled around languidly or lounged on plush cushions, in varying stages of beautifying themselves or tasting delicacies from far-away lands. Children of all ages ran past, all carrying a hint of David, most bearing the faces of different women. Gold, silver, and precious gems sparkled from every surface, especially from the women. Wisdom remembered designing those gems.

"Lord, I know You love him so, but how can you stand such blatant disobedience? So many women, who could have been loved by one man, tending their own homes? Not trapped here, vying for attention like petty children."

No answer came.

Wisdom wasn't expecting one, but the silence still hurt. She needed to get away. Spend time with Him.

Solomon stopped, cocked his head to the side. Wisdom stumbled to a halt before she ran into him, mindful of the effect she had on the creatures when she touched them.

He turned his head, looked up at her, and smiled.

"Solomon. Come."

Solomon trotted after his mother and took her outstretched hand.

Wisdom stared as the two hurried away. She swallowed.

He can see me? Here? Outside of my home?

Well, that was unexpected. This was going to be harder than she thought.

❈ ❈ ❈

Lust peeked around the corner, staring as Wisdom trailed the two creatures.

She was going to *kill* Folly the next time she saw her. Solomon hadn't left Wisdom's safety. Rather, Wisdom had followed him here like the plague that she was.

Lust sagged against the wall, relieved Wisdom kept moving and remained unaware of Lust's presence. She clenched her fists, one of her long nails snapping. She stared down at her formerly perfect, manicured nails in horror.

Oh, yes, Folly was going to pay. Big time.

"Lucifer, I simply cannot do it." Lust stared at the stone wall and cleared her throat. "Lucifer, there's been a misunderstanding. Folly..."

She grabbed her long blond strands and tugged—not too hard. She knew how difficult it was to remain beautiful while hair and skin and nails molted like they wanted to flee their owner. How difficult it was with the constant fire, the ice, the rot that permeated her life. She tried again.

"Lucifer, I have to tell you something."

"Tell me what?"

Lust spun, the smile springing to her face as if it had never been absent.

"Lucifer! Darling! I was just thinking of you!"

She ran to him and threw her arms around his neck, pressing herself tight against him.

"So I heard," he said blandly. "What is this about Folly?"

She waved her hand in the air, swiping the words away.

"Oh, nothing. Nothing at all. What are you doing here?"

He quirked an eyebrow.

"I've missed you," she quickly added.

"I've come to see your progress. It was quite brilliant, actually, your idea of seducing the son you thought would next be on the throne. However did you think of it?"

Lust laughed while she scrambled for something to say.

"Oh, you know, just did. Anyway, there he is and here I am! Now you've seen us, so goodbye."

Lust pushed him down the path, away from the boy and the *other* with him.

"Wait a moment." Lucifer dodged her shoving arms and stared through the wall. "Is that *Wisdom* with him?"

Lust sighed and, once again, slumped against the wall. "The one and the same."

He speared her with a frosty glare. "And how, may I ask, were you planning on getting past her?"

Lust threw up her hands and looked away. Lucifer was silent for too long, staring at the now-sleeping Solomon, Wisdom hovering over him like a new mother does her offspring.

"It looks like you need help."

Lust rolled her eyes. "And whom do you suggest I ask? No one will come when they find out Wisdom is guarding the boy."

Lucifer grinned, and Lust was at once repulsed and intrigued. Mostly repulsed.

"Me. And I suggest you ask nicely."

Lust sauntered over to him. Slowly. She dropped her voice to a sultry purr.

"Lucifer, darling, might you distract the pesky Wisdom for the teeniest, tiniest bit? I will make it worth your while, I promise."

Lucifer's eyes gleamed, their black depths flashing with desire. "Make it fast, and make it count."

She cocked her head to the side. "I've never heard you say that before."

She raised herself on her tiptoes and lifted her lips to his. He shoved her face away.

"Go."

She blinked back tears as her fingers traced the jagged slash he had left on her cheek. She patted at the congealing blood, wishing it would heal quickly—knowing it wouldn't.

She turned away from his retreating figure and watched Wisdom closely. Wisdom's head flew up, and she vanished from Solomon's side.

Crouching on the ground, one giant leap and Lust was at Solomon's side.

❊ ❊ ❊

Sweat trickled down Solomon's temple. He whimpered in his sleep. He swatted at the images playing in his mind, trying to push them away—trying to tug them closer.

Solomon bolted upright, the covers sliding from his small shoulders. Footsteps sounded from the hall. The curtain separating his room from his mother's was shoved aside.

"Solomon? I heard your cry—is everything ok? Are you ok?"

Bathsheba reached out to touch him, but he jerked away.

"Bad dream," he mumbled.

"Okay." Her hand dropped to her side. "Do you want me to stay with you?"

He shook his head and scooted farther away from her, not looking at her. After a few moments, she left, lingering at the doorway before letting the drapery fall from her fingers.

Relieved that she was gone, he tried to catch his breath; it still came in short gasps. He couldn't tell her about his dream. It was so — dirty. And, yet, he liked it.

He uneasily slid back into the sheets, replaying the images in his mind, telling himself he shouldn't.

But he did.

❂ ❂ ❂

Wisdom bolted through the wall, stopping short.

Solomon's eyes were shut, but his body was rigid, the blankets clutched in his tiny fists. She moved toward him, trying to sooth, wishing she could see what he saw.

One thing was certain. She could smell Lust's stench everywhere.

Wisdom came close and gently swiped the hair away from his forehead. He jerked away and gasped, sweat matting hair to skin. She frowned as she gazed down at the small boy.

What had Lust done to him?

Chapter Seventeen

Now the advice of Ahithophel, which he gave in those days, was as if one had inquired at the oracle of God. So was all the advice of Ahithophel both with David and with Absalom.
2 Samuel 16:23

"Ahithophel—" Wisdom started.

"No! You're either with me or against me. Which is it?"

Wisdom took a deep breath and glided toward the chair she had offered Ahithophel. She sat in the one next to it, sweeping her hand toward the still-vacant seat. Ahithophel remained standing.

"Ahithophel, I do not deny what David did was wrong. It was. Completely, absolutely, utterly wrong. But there are two things you are forgetting. One, David repented—he made things as right as he could —and Yahweh forgave him. Two, he is the Lord's anointed. He is to remain king of Israel until the Maker says otherwise."

Ahithophel's fists clenched. "I cannot respect a man like that."

"That may be, but what has Yahweh forgiven you of, dear one?"

"Not murder! Not adultery! David deserves worse than death—he deserves his kingdom ripped from him. He deserves to die, knowing his son—someone he loves and trusts—has betrayed him. He deserves to know I am the one who orchestrated every moment. And he deserves to stare at me from the end of my sword while I watch the life fade from his eyes."

"And that…would not be murder?"

Ahithophel stepped closer and thrust his chin forward.

"No. It would be justice."

Wisdom maintained eye contact. Her irate former student didn't flinch.

"You are right," she said quietly.

An eyebrow shot heavenward. His fists relaxed, if only slightly.

"You agree? Then you'll join me? Advise me?"

Wisdom stood, and, taking his fist into both of her hands, shook her head.

"No, dearest Ahithophel. Justice belongs to the Almighty, no one else. He is not asking you to do this thing. Wait on Him. Let Him lead you on the right path."

Ahithophel jerked away.

"My granddaughter was ruined by that man! Bathsheba is dead to our family. We no longer even speak of her. My grandson-in-law, Uriah—one of David's own men!—murdered. My first great-grandchild also murdered because of David's sins, according to the prophet Nathan. My son, Eliam can't even hold his head up among David's other mighty men, not after what David did to his daughter. It is time for Absalom to rule. Join us, Wisdom. We cannot fail with you to advise me—advise us all. David does not deserve to be king."

"No, he does not, but it is for the Maker to decide, not you. David has been forgiven, his sins covered by the blood offering he made. He is king."

"Well, he is no king of mine."

Turning, he stalked out the door, slamming it behind him.

Wisdom dropped her head and rubbed her eyes. "Oh, Ahithophel, why won't you listen?"

"My lady? Are you opening your school again?"

Wisdom's head jerked up.

"Ella! What are you doing here?"

The young angel clasped her hands.

"Forgive me. I saw your student, then I saw you return, and I was hoping..." Her voice trailed off, and she shrugged. "You know."

Wisdom smiled. "I do. And I'm very, very sorry. I only came to help Solomon's great-grandfather. I should return to the palace."

Ella sighed. "Yes, ma'am."

Wisdom laid her hand on the girl's shoulder.

"Would you do me a favor, Ella? Would you check on Hakeem? See how he fares? I would love a report. And I'm sure he could use your help in some way."

Ella's eyes brightened. "I would love to! Thank you so much!"

She darted away, excitement painting every movement of her flight.

Wisdom chuckled, then turned to watch Ahithophel ride away on his horse. Sadness filled her. He was so intent on seeing to David's destruction. And yet David's downfall would be his own.

Her shoulders drooped. David had been warned. Bloodshed would not depart from his family. Now he would see that firsthand. He may have been forgiven, but the consequences of his sin—beginning with the death of Bathsheba's first child—had only begun.

❊ ❊ ❊

After checking to make sure Solomon was safe, Wisdom flew for the palace. He and Bathsheba may have been wearied by their escape from Jerusalem, but they were perfectly safe. For now.

Wisdom reached the palace just before Ahithophel.

Ahithophel entered the council's chamber and bowed before Absalom.

"My king."

"Ahithophel. I have done as you suggested. What next?"

Hatred poisoned the air around Ahithophel. Wisdom shuddered. This was not what she wanted for him. Not ever. She listened as he advised Absalom.

"You have slept with David's concubines—you have established you are king in your father's place. Now, quickly, before it is too late, let me choose 12,000 men and chase David while he is tired and discouraged. I will harm no one else—I will kill only the king—and lead the rest of your people back into the city for you to rule."

Absalom and the rest of his council murmured their agreement. Ahithophel had helped Absalom seize power faster than any of them had dreamed possible.

Wisdom's shoulder's drooped. Ahithophel had such a keen mind. He and Solomon were so much alike. Everything she taught they both grasped with astounding clarity. Even now. Ahithophel's counsel was sound. Everything he said was correct. But David was not done being king. The Maker had been very clear.

Or so she had heard from Hushai, one of the counselors.

Wisdom squirmed. She should have heard it from the Maker Himself. She would talk to Him about it later. Right after she finished protecting Solomon. Absalom would surely have Solomon put to death if Absalom became king. She focused on what Hushai was saying.

"Absalom, O king, live forever. David is a warrior, and he is furious. If you attack now, he and his mighty men will overwhelm your soldiers and defeat you immediately. You need to call for backup from the farthest regions of your country. You can't lose to him now, not when we're so close."

Ahithophel started to speak. Absalom turned away, and the counselors leaned together, whispering with Absalom. Ahithophel frowned at Hushai.

Hushai was David's friend, sent by the king to confound Ahithophel's counsel. A traitor. Not one of them suspected. The council pulled apart, Absalom speaking.

"Let's do that. That sounds so much better than what Ahithophel said. Quickly, send runners to the outer provinces. Gather my army."

Ahithophel's eyes widened. "Your majesty, I—"

Absalom lifted a hand, silencing him.

"I'm beginning to question your loyalty, Ahithophel. Tell me, do you wish us to succeed?"

Ahithophel snapped his mouth closed and bowed.

"I have no king but you, sire."

Absalom nodded, but he didn't look convinced. Ahithophel turned and strode from the chamber.

Wisdom smiled, her eyes sad.

The Lord had defeated Ahithophel's good advice. Disaster waited for Absalom.

❀ ❀ ❀

Folly waited for Ahithophel.

He burst from the council room, steps pounding, chest heaving, fists clenched. She grinned. Perfect. She stayed hidden in an alcove until she was certain Wisdom had left.

She stepped from hiding right before he passed her.

"Ahithophel."

He paused.

"Poor Ahithophel," she purred. "The king wouldn't listen to you? You know what that means, right? Absalom will fail. Your life is forfeit."

His fists clenched tighter. His knuckles turned white.

"There's only one thing to do. Make it impossible for David to have the satisfaction of ending your life."

Ahithophel rubbed his neck.

"That's right. It's hopeless. David will never forgive you. Besides, you couldn't allow him to rule over you anyway."

Ahithophel grunted and marched away, determination in every stride.

Folly laughed. Oh, it was just too easy.

❀ ❀ ❀

Wisdom stood next to Ahithophel.

Waited for the wooden beam to stop creaking. For the rope to slow its swinging. Eyes rolled back, his life force slowly faded from his earthly vessel and reappeared next to Wisdom.

They both stared at the too-still form hanging from the end of a rope.

Death took a step forward.

Wisdom held out her hand. "Not yet."

Death sneered. "You can't deny me what's mine."

Wisdom grasped the hilt of her sword and pulled it out halfway. She stepped forward, eyes blazing.

Death scrambled backward. He crossed his arms.

168

"I'll wait right here, then. By all means, proceed."

Wisdom scowled and sheathed her sword.

"You will wait outside."

Death shrugged. "As you wish."

He strolled outside the dwelling, in no hurry at all. He cast one leering grin over his shoulder at Ahithophel before the wooden wall separated them. Wisdom followed his gaze to Ahithophel.

Ahithophel trembled, staring after Death with a pale face.

"Who—who was that?"

"Death."

"And—he said—he said—I'm his?"

Wisdom nodded, her heart breaking.

"But why? I did what was right! I did what needed to be done!"

"You did what was right in your own eyes, Ahithophel. You didn't do what the Maker wanted you to do. You didn't call on Him to help you. To avenge you. You sought the destruction of the Lord's anointed and held fast to your path until the very end. It didn't have to end like this."

Ahithophel clasped both of her hands in his.

"I'm sorry! I—I didn't realize… Take me with you. I don't want to go with that—*thing*. Please. Give me a chance to explain to Yahweh. He will understand. I know He will."

Wisdom shook her head and gently extracted her hands from his.

"You will see the Maker, but I'm afraid you won't like what He has to say. Oh, Ahithophel, my Ahithophel! I tried so very hard to warn you! To turn you away from this choice. I love you so, and I am so very sorry it had to end this way."

"No. No!"

Wisdom beckoned with her hand. Death slid through the wall without his consent. A storm gathered on his face.

"I am not some puppet to be called whenever you wish," he hissed.

"Please, no, Wisdom. Please," Ahithophel pleaded.

Tears filled her eyes, and she ignored Death.

"I wanted you to know why," she whispered.

Death wrapped a talon-clad hand around Ahithophel's arm.

"I have so much to show you, pest. You are gonna hate it."

Wisdom's eyes snapped fire. "But first you will take him to the Maker! He will decide Ahithophel's fate, not you."

Death flinched away from the powerful flame he glimpsed in her being, then glared at Wisdom.

"As you wish, *craftsman*."

Wisdom bristled. How could he make her beloved profession sound like such an insult? They matched glare for glare. She shooed him away.

"Be gone with you, foul beast."

Death grinned, but his expression held no mirth.

"And I was so beginning to enjoy your company."

Wisdom scowled. "The Lord rebuke you!"

Death stumbled back, then grasped Ahithophel's arm tighter. He unfurled skeletal wings and moved away from Wisdom as swiftly as he could. Ahithophel's pitiful cries pulled Wisdom out of her scowl.

"Ahithophel…"

She watched Death escort him to heaven. Before the clouds enveloped him, Death cast a triumphant grin over his shoulder. Wisdom shook her head. Death was so certain of the outcome.

Mercy, Lord. Please have mercy.

Silence.

Wisdom bit back a sob.

She needed to check on Solomon.

※ ※ ※

Solomon and his mother were somber as they came back into the city.

Bathsheba's eyes darted around the thoroughfare, searching faces, looking for her grandfather. For Ahithophel.

Wisdom's heart grieved. Bathsheba would be heartbroken when she discovered what had happened to him. Even though he hadn't spoken to her in many years. Since *that* year.

Bathsheba tugged on Solomon's arm. He bent and listened to what she had to say. He straightened. Wisdom watched, wanting to speak with Solomon. Now wasn't the time. Solomon's jaw was hard. Set. Bathsheba wanted Solomon's help to find Ahithophel. Solomon did not share his mother's feelings for the man who shunned her. The man who betrayed his own great-grandson, who plotted to take his king's life.

Drawing a cloak over her lush curls, Bathsheba darted away before they reached the palace gates. Solomon spoke to the soldiers guarding the king's wives, distracting them for his mother.

Solomon looked pointedly to Wisdom then to Bathsheba. Wisdom nodded and followed the figure flitting through the alleyways.

They came to Ahithophel's home. The front door stood ajar.

Pushing the wooden door open, Bathsheba stole inside. Her breath caught, fear shallowing her breathing. Had David already sent men to kill her grandfather for his betrayal? Voices led her to an inner chamber.

Wisdom trudged behind, knowing what Bathsheba would find, wishing she could keep the awful sight from her beloved's mother.

Bathsheba peeked around the corner, gasped, and ran forward. "Grandfather!"

Wisdom stepped into the room.

"Do not touch him!"

Eliam caught Bathsheba's wrists before she threw herself over Ahithophel's corpse. She struggled in vain.

"Let me go! Let me go to him!"

"It's too late. He's gone."

Bathsheba stilled, realizing who held her. She stared up at her father, tears in her eyes.

"You—you are speaking to me?"

He shoved her away, averting his eyes. He did not answer.

"Daddy, please—"

"You have no father."

Bathsheba stumbled back. She had been told the same thing before, but the pain was even more achingly real than when she had been found to be with child. David's child, not her husband's. Not

Uriah's child.

She glanced around the room. Her grandfather's corpse lay on the kitchen table, his face puffy, a cut rope tied to the rafters. Her mother stood behind the body weeping, her hands covering her face.

Bathsheba's two brothers wouldn't look at her either. The eldest, jaw clenched, stared straight ahead. The other, head down, jaw working. They had been so close.

"Mother?"

"You have no mother either."

Her father's voice was clipped. Her mother's sobs grew in volume.

"I see," she whispered. She glanced to Ahithophel's bloated corpse. "My grandfather denied me as well, and yet I am queen. You will not stop me from praying over him — from saying farewell."

She moved toward Ahithophel's remains. Her father matched her stride, eyes still averted. She smiled gently.

"Do not worry. I will not touch him. David would not want me to be unclean."

A low growl left Eliam's throat at the mention of her husband's name.

She moved close and whispered a prayer over her grandfather.

Someone cleared his throat.

Bathsheba glanced at the doorway. Benaiah, one of David's mighty men, stood within. Ignoring the rest in the room, Benaiah stared at Eliam.

"The king asks for you. Asks for your pledge of loyalty."

Eliam's jaw hardened.

"Do I not even get to bury my father first?"

Benaiah measured Eliam with his eyes, looking wary.

"If you wish for the king to further question your loyalties."

Eliam ground his teeth but gave a short bow. He had no choice. Benaiah outranked him.

"I will attend the king immediately." Eliam focused on his two sons. "See to your grandfather, then purify yourselves." He turned back to Benaiah. "I am ready."

Benaiah nodded, then focused on Bathsheba. Wisdom moved closer to her, though she knew Bathsheba had nothing to fear from the kind warrior. Benaiah, still ignoring the others in the room, bowed.

"My lady. Allow me to escort you to the palace."

Bathsheba dropped her gaze; her smile was strained.

"I do not believe my father wishes to be seen with me."

Benaiah didn't hesitate. "Your father knows his way to the palace, my queen. Your safety is my priority."

Bathsheba stared at her father, silently begging him to look at her, to acknowledge her one last time before she was locked away in the harem for the rest of her days.

He averted his gaze. The rest of her family turned their backs.

Cheeks burning, Bathsheba swept past her father, forcing herself not to cry or take one last look at her grandfather. She only hoped Eliam would support Solomon when he became king, as both the Lord and David had promised her.

Wisdom touched her shoulder as she passed.

"Solomon will be king, Bathsheba. Your mourning will turn to joy. I promise."

Bathsheba took a deep breath and slowly released it. Peace filled her.

"Do not give up on your family, my love. It is my every intention to be sure you see them again, in a place abounding with forgiveness."

A hint of a smile graced Bathsheba's lovely face.

Chapter Eighteen

"Just as I swore to you by the Lord God of Israel, saying, 'Assuredly Solomon your son shall be king after me, and he shall sit on my throne in my place,' so I certainly will do this day."
1 Kings 1:30

Wisdom followed Solomon — now a young man — down the passage. His shoulders drooped. His steps were heavy.

"It will be all right," Wisdom whispered.

He paused, his hand splayed against the thick wooden door separating him from his destiny. He was quiet a long moment.

"Thank you."

He pushed the door open, muscles straining his shirt.

Wisdom realized a moment too late that her eyes lingered on the corded muscle visible through his fine linen shirt. She snapped her eyes away and took a deep breath. Solomon had grown handsome indeed. Too handsome. More so than any other creature she had had the pleasure of knowing.

And she knew him well. Their long talks, the way he soaked in everything she said — then actually *did* it — endeared him to her as no other. She looked forward to the kind of rule he would have after his father David relocated to heaven.

The open door revealed King David, spent in years, laboring for each breath.

Abishag, the young concubine selected to lie close to the king — the physician's hope that her body heat would transfer to the king and extend his life — rose from her knees and stepped away as Solomon entered. A blush stained her features.

Wisdom shook her head, bewildered at the creatures' solution. What would they come up with next? David had not responded to the special "treatment." He had only grown more feeble as the days progressed.

Solomon's eyes followed the beautiful young woman as she slipped from the room. Wisdom nudged him and he turned toward his father.

"You've come."

The weak voice barely penetrated the furs draped across David's emaciated body.

"I have, Father."

"Good. Not—much time. I will soon rest with my fathers," he wheezed. "But I will see you crowned—before I go. Where is your mother?"

"I am here."

Bathsheba stepped closer to the bed from her silent vigil. He grasped her hand and squeezed, though it looked like he hadn't at all.

"Remember, always remember, I have loved you more than any other."

Bathsheba nodded solemnly, tears glistening on her cheeks.

Wisdom kept from rolling her eyes by the sheerest of willpower. If Love had forgiven all—the murder, the lust, the adultery—then she had no choice but to do the same. Solomon, the Maker's chosen heir, had come from the union, bringing something beautiful out of the worst sort of ugliness. Joy out of mourning. Beauty from ashes. Peace from despair.

But Wisdom still saw what could have been. The blueprint the Maker designed for them Himself. The king's weak voice interrupted her tangent.

"And Nathan?"

"Here, sire."

The prophet came close, standing at Solomon's side.

Two more men drifted out of the shadows, standing on the other side of the bed. Wisdom instantly recalled their names. Zadok the priest and Benaiah, one of David's mighty warriors.

The king lifted trembling fingers, stretching them toward Solomon. David's voice grew strong with determination.

"Quickly, this is what you must do so Adonijah, your brother, does not take the kingdom from you."

Two angels drifted through the wall and stood on either side of the king. Wisdom recognized their rank immediately. Sentries. Sent to guard the faithful's last moments on earth before escorting the creatures to their palaces, making those last moments ones of rest and peace.

"Surely it isn't time yet?" she blurted.

The two glanced at each other.

"Don't you know?" one asked.

A flush swept across Wisdom's face even as she tried to staunch its tidal wave. She should know. She sputtered, unable to form an explanation.

The other looked at her kindly. "Wisdom. Don't you think it's time for a visit?"

Her eyes flew to Solomon, who was listening intently to his father's plans.

"Don't worry. He'll be safe. I'll see to it."

Shame gushed over Wisdom under their expectant gazes.

"I can't. He needs me, especially once his father leaves. Besides..." Her voice trailed away.

How could she say what started as busyness had morphed into avoidance? How could she go back before every creature had turned his or her heart to the Maker? How could she leave her Solomon, now, in his direst time, when he knew not whether he would live through his brother's plotting?

"Go on. He misses you."

Her gaze snapped to the first angel who spoke. The corner of his mouth quirked, and he nodded.

Then she was hurtling.

Out of the room, through the ceiling, past the skies, the clouds, the birds. Through the empty void of space, past the brilliant stars.

Soaring higher, faster.

Up and over the pearl gates, into the King's country, toward the palace — the very throne room of God. His heart drew her to Him like a beacon.

She plowed into the antechamber she had built to the side of His throne room. He stood, His back to her, surrounded by creatures and angels.

He turned just as she reached Him.

She threw herself at Him, into His arms. His arms clasped tight around her. She heard a few chuckles, but she didn't care. She felt, rather than saw, the angels ushering everyone else out of the room. She glanced over her shoulder.

Moses, Abraham, Enoch — Aurik, Káel, Raphael, and more — it had been too long since she had spoken to any of them. The door closed gently behind them.

They were alone.

Wisdom's heart squeezed, and she buried her face in His neck, suddenly afraid of what she would see when she looked into His eyes. Those wonderful, captivating, heart-rending eyes.

"Wisdom."

She clung tighter. He gently disentangled her arms from around His neck.

"It is good to see you, My love."

She stepped back and ducked her head, scuffing her turquoise slipper on the floor swirling with color. Inexplicably shy. She hadn't felt this way around Him before. She had always known she was welcome, anytime. Welcome to just — *be* with him.

He held out His hand.

"Come, let us talk."

She gingerly took his fingertips and trailed Him to the crystal bench that shared the floor's lightning strikes of color. The bench they had spent countless hours on, designing and redesigning every aspect of the planet He spoke into being. When they weren't traveling the galaxies, that is. The planet she had crafted at the speed of light — faster, even — as His Spirit had pulled something out of nothing. Creating matter for her to form, to mold, to shape into something wonderful. The sparkling globe at her feet.

But the creatures were all Him.

His design, His creation, His breath — her dust.

She stared at it all in wonder. It had been too long.

"How is Solomon?"

She soaked in His voice, not even realizing until this moment how lost she had been without Him.

"Oh, he is wonderful! But…"

A frown marred her pristine face.

"Yes, My love?"

She turned to Him.

"I'm afraid — so very afraid for him. He listens to what I say, but there is a part of himself he keeps hidden from me — a part I cannot heal if he won't let me."

A fiery white eyebrow rose.

"That *you* cannot heal?"

Wisdom stared at Him, her lips parted.

"That I can't —"

She groaned and dropped her head into her hands.

"No *wonder* I've been having so much trouble! I've been trying to fix everything!" She peeked up at Him and crinkled her forehead. "Forgive me?"

He nodded, face solemn, eyes twinkling.

"Of course. I've missed you, you know."

"And I You." Wisdom shook her head. "I can't believe I waited so long — never mind. It's over, done, forgiven, and in the past."

The King nodded His agreement, His smile tugging at His mouth.

She looked up at Him, her smile radiant.

"How have you been?"

His smile crept across His face and thrilled her to her very toes.

"I thought you'd never ask."

☼ ☼ ☼

The screams followed her.

"I didn't mean to kill him! I was just so angry!"

"Come on, there's gotta be a second chance! Please, somebody, give me a second chance!"

"I was a good person; why am I here? Help me. Help me!"

The rest were guttural moans, cries, shrieks, wails. The unyielding sounds of torment.

Folly clamped her hands over her ears and ran.

The more ghosts who filled the cavern deep below terra's crust, the harder it was to get away from the constant agony. The weak beings couldn't even take it as the angels had. At least *they* had regrouped, pushed past the pain, the fire, the ice, their hatred for one another, intent on toppling the maker himself. These pathetic ghouls couldn't function past the torture they were enduring. Which made Folly despise them even more.

She stumbled to a halt.

I have been through worse than you, longer than you, and look at me!

She spread her hands wide and glared at the closest soul.

The woman, chained to the floor with glowing, red-hot chains, screamed and huddled away from Folly, straining at the chains that smoked with sizzling skin.

Folly looked down at herself—saw the hideous beast she had become.

She snarled and slashed at the woman with her claws, only wanting her to *shut up.*

Blood ruptured into red ribbons down the woman's face, but her cries of terror only grew in volume. Folly cried out and grabbed her own head, the woman's voice bouncing inside her skull, growing in intensity.

She bolted down the tunnel.

I'll do it! I'll take Lucifer's next assignment—wherever it is—whoever it is! Just as long as it's away from here!

She bolted into the first chamber she came to, ran toward the wall, and crouched near it, not daring to touch the frozen, boiling surface. Her knees pressed into her chest; she squeezed her eyes shut. She rocked on the balls of her feet, too weary to sit. Trying to block the noise. The voices.

Everything went silent.

She stilled.

Her eyes drifted open.

Her gasp stuck in her throat. She rose to her feet, slowly, afraid to shatter the stillness.

She was in heaven.

And it was completely silent. No one stirred. It was just her and the peaceful scene before her. No one else.

She soaked it all in. The lush, rolling hills. The crystalline castle reaching its spires high into the clouds. The clear-gold path, wending its way from under her feet to the palace beyond. The vibrant Tree of Life resting next to the luminous River of Life, which flowed from the throne of God.

Her eyes caught and held onto the tree.

She had wondered what had happened to it after the flood.

A tear traced its way down her cheek. And then another. Then another. Tears dripped onto her clothes, her hands, her feet. Still she made not a sound.

She took one step, then another. The path wasn't as solid as she remembered it. It sank under each step she took, but she couldn't take her eyes off the beauty before her to see why. Colors she didn't remember existed danced before her. Not a hint of darkness — black, gray, death — anywhere.

Her feet halted next to the tree and its glistening fruit. Gold, silver, purple, red, blue, orange — she stopped counting. Twelve different fruits. Twelve varied colors. Love, joy, peace — fruit she hadn't tasted in millennia — longer, it seemed.

She reached out, hesitated. She couldn't wait a moment more. Her hand darted out, snatching a lush fruit. She bit into it as one starved.

It powdered in her mouth.

She choked on the dust, the fruit's ripe scent snuffed out like a flame. She stared in bewilderment at the charred remains drifting through her hands.

She grabbed another fruit, desperate to taste it.

It disintegrated before it reached her mouth.

She started ripping fruit from the Tree, frantic to relish just one bite. Each turned into silt as she touched them.

She stumbled as she stretched higher to reach the disappearing fruit. She grabbed a branch for support.

The tree shrank away from her, gnarled and black—the leaves and fruit powdering in the wind.

A tear fell from her cheek. She tracked its descent, impossibly slow, as it plummeted toward a flower. A brilliant, breathtaking, red hibiscus.

She swiped at it too late. It struck the flower, bringing instant death.

Black veins spidered from under her feet, infecting the ground.

She stepped back, whispering "No," just wanting it to stop.

It didn't.

"No," she said a little louder, still afraid to break the eerie calm.

The sweet air caressing her nose turned rancid. She gagged, waving the venom away from her face. The putrid air drifted away, poisoning everything it touched.

She bit back her cry, not wanting to make it worse.

She took another step back and stumbled. Folly looked down.

Everywhere she stepped, the ground crumbled. Turned black. Died.

Dark spider webs forced their way out of each footstep, racing toward the celestial city.

Dwellings started to crumble.

Folly's gaze darted around desperately. She only wanted to make it stop. To fix it. Somehow.

The darkest, ugliest vein of them all, barreled straight toward the palace, cracking ground and flinging it away as it raced toward the crystal structure. The poison contaminated the rest of the landscape, dulling everything in sight.

Folly had to stop it.

She flung herself toward the end of the cancer eating and destroying the loveliness. She had to fix what she had done. Repair what she had broken. She tried to fly, but her wings failed her.

She charged across the landscape.

Reaching the end of the vein, she strained for it, intent on catching it—stopping it. It exploded away from her, right into the palace walls.

The castle shattered, the clamor of breaking glass deafening. The spires, far above the land, dropped out of sight, swallowed by the hungry ground.

The glass struck her like the blast of a sandstorm, but far worse.

But she couldn't look away.

The ground devoured the broken palace, and anything remaining above melted like molten lead, fusing into gray, lifeless lumps.

The grinding destruction settled into silence. Nothing moved. Everything was dead.

Folly pivoted slowly, taking it all in. Not one vibrant color remained.

The ground was jagged, torn. A gnarled tree. A dry, cracked creek bed. Ruins. Destruction. Molten lead.

She staggered in a complete circle and faced where the palace had been. Only the remains weren't there.

The ruins were far away, and the Maker stood in the empty space. In the midst of the decay.

He didn't say a word. Just looked at her. Sad. Compassionate. Torn. Caring.

With sudden clarity, she knew.

This is what she had done to earth. To His creatures.

"I'm so sorry," she whispered.

He didn't move—didn't acknowledge He had heard her.

"Didn't you hear me? I said I'm sorry! I'm so sorry!"

She was shouting, screaming—trying to make Him hear her. But her voice fell to the ground at her feet.

Then He was gone.

"Nooooo!"

The scream ripped from her chest. She couldn't make it stop. She lifted her face to the broiling sky and screamed and screamed.

Chapter Nineteen

"Get wisdom! Get understanding! Do not forget, nor turn away from the words of my mouth. Do not forsake her, and she will preserve you; love her, and she will keep you."
Proverbs 4:5-6

"She's awake!"

Folly's eyes sprang open. Her cheek stung.

Religion, inches from her face, had his hand raised and was staring at her with wide eyes. He seemed reluctant to drop his hand, but he did anyway. Other faces hovered above her, and they all looked frightened. Even Lucifer. Especially Lucifer.

"What did you see, Folly?"

His voice was strong, belying the terror in his eyes.

Her eyes rolled as she stared around the room, trying to take it all in. One second, she was *there*; the next, back here. The one place she had thought worse than all others. The one place she didn't think could compete with any other for the agony of its existence. But there was a worse place. Heaven—destroyed.

Tremors shook her, and she fisted her hands, trying to make them stop.

"Death! Give her something!"

Her mind grasped for something solid. Remembering what drove her to this obscure room. Right. Running, trying to escape the tormented souls who wouldn't let her go. Then...*that.*

She closed her eyes, only wanting to block all she had seen.

The voices fluctuated around her in snarls and grunts, but she pushed them away. She just wanted them to leave. Rough hands dragged her into sitting. She opened her eyes as Death pushed his way through those thronged around her. Her mind barely registered him as he hunkered down before her. She still saw veins full of poison — killing, destroying.

He forced her mouth open. She half-heartedly resisted, weakly tugging her face away, almost wondering what he was doing. He gripped her face tighter. Wedging a flask between her lips, he upended it.

Folly gagged and jerked away, spewing the noxious yellow goo on those closest.

Cries and curses followed, but Folly didn't care. She only wanted the vile liquid *out*.

Forcing her head back, Death plugged her nose and poured the rest of the contents down her throat. Choking, she fought, prying his hands off her, but he didn't let go until the poison snaked its way down Folly's throat.

Her throat burned as the acid scorched it. It ignited a trail of heat down to her stomach, and her stomach revolted.

Jumping to her feet, Folly doubled over and retched until nothing more would come. It sizzled as it splattered, going up in acrid smoke.

Death cursed and moved away, but soon came back, another flask in his hands. She held up her hand and gasped for breath as he came toward her.

"Touch me again, and I'll tell the next angel where you keep the keys to this awful place."

His surprise was fleeting, quickly replaced by a smile that didn't reach his eyes.

"Oh, you would, would you? You don't even know where I keep them."

Folly shrugged, not saying a word. She didn't have to. Death was paranoid enough to take her threat seriously. He stroked those keys obsessively when he thought no one was looking. Why Lucifer entrusted him with the keys to the prisoner's bonds, she would never know—

"Enough of this! What did you see?" Lucifer demanded. "You were asleep for three days. *Asleep*. Like the creatures go to sleep. That is unheard of—we don't sleep! Is something wrong with you? You must have seen something. What was it?"

Folly's eyes darted around the room while her mind scrambled for something to say. The vision was too fresh in her mind—too bleeding—too raw for her to share. Yet. If ever.

Lucifer took a step closer.

Her mind grabbed hold of something.

"The son!" she blurted.

Everyone stared at her. The color drained from Lucifer's face.

Folly tried to get her mind to work. Her mouth to form words. To forget the other vision, if only for a little while.

"Here."

"Here," Lucifer repeated. "With us?"

At his thunderous look, Folly rushed on.

"In chains. Disgraced. We get to torture him."

Glee erupted on every face except one.

"Truly, Folly?" gurgled Famine, her face uglier with her smile than without.

Folly nodded but kept her eyes on Lucifer.

"Get out."

The other fallen angels obeyed Lucifer, taking their time. Celebrating. Making plans. All too thrilled with the good news to notice he wasn't happy.

Death lingered, shamelessly eavesdropping as he stood just outside the open doorway. Folly glared at him, but he smiled back, his white eyes softly glowing in the darkness.

Lucifer came close and leaned forward, dropping his voice. "You screamed, 'No!' for almost an entire day."

Her eyes flew wide. "You—you wouldn't let me help. Torment him, I mean."

"You said, 'I'm sorry.'"

Her mind scrambled. "I—I was begging your forgiveness. So you would let me. Help."

He leaned closer. "I don't believe you," he whispered.

He held her gaze for an eternity.

She trembled, unable to break the gaze, unable to force any other words out of her constricting throat. Fear enveloped her—just as it did him—and still he stared.

Spinning, he swept out of the door. Folly sucked in a full breath and collapsed against the wall, oblivious to the pain the wall seared into her flesh.

Death peeked around the corner and captured her gaze, holding it for too long a moment. His eyes held a promise. Of what, she didn't know, but she was certain she never wanted to find out.

Sweat dripped from her forehead, running in rivulets down the sides of her face. The longer she was trapped here, the worse her enemies became.

✾ ✾ ✾

"Wisdom! My father sends me to be anointed king!"

He ran to her and clasped her hands in his.

"That's wonderful, Solomon—"

She was still basking in the Lord's glory. His next words slammed into her without warning.

"Marry me," he blurted, interrupting her.

"Wha—what?"

"Marry me."

He gently, tenderly kissed the backs of her hands. His fervent eyes held pleading.

"I need you with me more than ever. I don't know how to be king! How to rule—how to lead. I need you—and the Lord—to show me how to walk, how to stand. I need you—"

Wisdom snatched her hands away and stumbled back, his words finally penetrating her stupor.

"Solomon!"

His grin stretched wide as he gestured toward the palace

surrounding them.

"You can live here with me, instead of at the Lord's side in heaven."

"Solomon, you don't know what you say!"

He laughed, his joy ringing through the chamber and out to the terrace beyond.

"Don't worry. I will ask the Lord for your hand. He has promised to lead me—to prosper me, but I know it will be so much better with you at my side." He came to her, gazed at her with all the passion of a man in love. He lifted his hand, and his fingers trailed the side of her face. "Say yes, my love. Say yes."

Tears filled Wisdom's eyes, but they did not fall.

"You don't know what you ask." She strangled out the hoarse whisper.

One tear fell.

He swiped it away and chuckled. "Of course I do."

She shook her head. "No, Solomon, you don't."

"I'll ask anyway."

He kissed her. One light, feathery touch. His lips barely grazing hers. Then he was gone.

She watched him leave, her heart pounding within her.

Then she was barreling. Barreling through the roof, into the sky, straight for the tallest mountain. Tears streaming, heart breaking, she tore through the air. One beat of her wings, and she rested on the highest mountaintop.

Landing on the mountain with a poof of powdery snow spraying into the air, she screamed. She screamed again and again. Looking to the sky, tears streamed down her face and she fell silent.

"Maker." Her voice barely wafted past her mouth. "I need you."

And she was in His arms.

She sobbed as He held her, stroking her hair, her back, her wings.

"Is this a test?" She hiccuped. "Do you test me?"

His hands spread peace throughout her, but her heart still shuddered in pain.

"Do you love him?"

She pulled back, staring at Him with wide eyes.

"Of course I do! More than any other who has walked before him! He listens to me."

The Maker smiled tenderly. "It is why I love him too. You didn't answer Me. Do you love him?"

She tilted her head and stared at Him. She *had* just answered Him. Then it crept into her heart what He truly asked. She buried her face in Love's garment.

"I could never give You up for him. Never." She groaned. "Why is this so difficult? I wanted to help him, not hinder him! Oh, Solomon."

She grieved for the precious man far below her, who, *yes*, she admitted to herself, a life with him would be pleasant, even for the wisp of time the creatures now stayed on the planet.

"Do you want to marry him, Wisdom?"

Wisdom stared at Him, shocked.

She shook her head no, then stopped. Slowly, she nodded.

"Do you love him?"

She nodded again.

"I—I'm not sure how it happened, Master, but—yes. I do." She stared at Him, each tear reflecting the glistening snowflakes that hovered around the pair. She raised her chin. "But there is something You have that he could never give me."

"And what is that?"

"You. Your love."

His smile warmed her.

She had to ask.

"Is—is there a way?"

They had this conversation long ago. But it had meant nothing to Wisdom then. She hadn't been able to fathom why an angel would choose a creature over the Maker. Now she knew.

"Not without disobeying Me. Not without—separation."

Her gaze pinged to those wallowing in their fallen state.

"It isn't worth it."

"No, it isn't. I'm so sorry, My love."

She stood back and rubbed her arms, her eyes seeking Solomon's form far below her.

The King's gaze followed her own. "Even now he asks for you."

She shuddered and slammed her eyes closed.

"Would you—would you tell him for me? Please? I don't think I can face him again, not after…"

Her voice trailed off, and she lifted her fingertips to her lips.

Love gently took her hand and kissed her cheek. His eyes were compassionate. She lifted trembling lips, trying to smile. He kissed her again and was gone.

Rubbing her arms against a chill that had nothing to do with the snowflakes, she watched their conversation, leaning forward without knowing it.

❊ ❊ ❊

"Oh, Lord God Almighty, Maker of heaven and earth!"

Falling to his knees, then his face, Solomon launched into a lengthy and eloquent prayer.

Ten minutes passed.

"So you see why I, the most humble of men, must beg of you for Wisdom's hand in marriage."

A smile played about the Lord's lips.

"That was quite some prayer."

A smug grin quirked the corners of Solomon's mouth.

"Thank you."

The Master turned serious.

"It is a compliment that you love her so, but I cannot allow you to be married."

"But…but, why not, my Lord? I have done all you asked—I have followed your precepts, kept your word, and followed the laws of my father, David. You gave me Wisdom when I first asked for her, but, now she's done with my teaching, I want her by my side for the rest of my days! Didn't you ordain marriage? Didn't you say it was good for a man to leave his father and mother…"

The King held up His hand. Solomon held his tongue. Barely.

"Solomon, you don't know what you are asking. I have seen your admiration for her, but I want you to look at Me the way you look at her. Your worship and love belong to Me alone, not to Wisdom."

The King shook His head when Solomon spread his hands and opened his mouth.

"Solomon, I'm going to tell you a story. Perhaps you'll understand. Before the days of the great flood, many angels took wives for themselves among the daughters of men, even though I told them not to. Powerful creatures were born. Some gigantic, some incredibly smart, fast, strong—and full of far more evil than any of My creatures could imagine on their own. They taught My creatures their wickedness, and killed and hurt many of them, enslaving them."

Solomon sputtered.

"I know, I know, My love. That would never happen to you, and you would teach your offspring to love Me as much as you do."

Solomon nodded in satisfaction.

"The thing is, your children will have a choice. They choose whether they love Me or don't. I can't allow super-human creatures to once again turn hearts away from me, or hurt great masses of My creatures—My humans—again."

Solomon stood rigid. "Does Wisdom have a choice in this?"

The King nodded. "She does. But I think you will find her answer the same as before."

"I would like to ask her. Please."

The *please* sounded like an afterthought.

"You would go against Me in this?"

Solomon blanched. He cleared his throat.

"N—no, Sir. I just—I thought I could, well, you know, maybe—"

"Change My mind?"

Solomon swallowed hard. "Well, um, yes."

The King smiled. "You won't."

Solomon looked down and breathed a heavy sigh.

"Can't I at least ask her?"

Love shook His head. Always so stubborn. Always so adamant to get their own way.

"I will send her in."

Turning, He left Solomon's antechamber.

* * *

Wisdom could see Solomon's self-satisfied smile.

"You heard?"

Wisdom took a deep breath. "I did, Master."

"And?"

Wisdom reared back, mouth open. "I can't believe You'd have to ask again, my Lord. *Of course* I wouldn't go against You!"

Seconds ticked away. Solomon looked impatient.

"Do you care for him, My Wisdom?"

Unexpected tears filled Wisdom's eyes. She studied Solomon's strong form, his regal bearing.

"You know I do. He is perhaps the most beautiful creature you have made yet. None compare to him, not even his father, David. And he listens to me." She looked at Him with wide eyes. "Do you know how rare that is?"

His eyes crinkled at the corners. "I do."

"I could spend the rest of my days loving him. But there is just one thing I could never get past."

"And what is that, dearest Wisdom?"

She stared at Him earnestly, fervently. "He could never love me as much as You do. I could never give You up for him."

The King nodded once. "Thank you, Wisdom. Your words mean a great deal to Me." He nodded toward Solomon. "I'll be close by if you need Me. I do not envy you your task."

He faded from sight. She stared at Solomon with trepidation.

"Nor do I."

* * *

"Folly, I have an assignment for you."

Folly moved forward, standing before the garish throne that towered above her. For once, she wished she could remain completely invisible to Lucifer.

She glanced at Lust, who, perched on one of the claw-like armrests, draped her arm possessively across Lucifer's shoulders. She smiled sweetly at Folly. Too sweetly.

Folly scowled at Lust. Crossing her arms, she faced Lucifer defiantly.

"What is it?"

"Wisdom."

A beat.

She shook her head, certain she had heard wrong.

"Excuse me, did you say—Wisdom?"

The voices in the room blended together, creating a loud buzz in her ears. Lucifer nodded once.

"I'm sorry—how is Wisdom an assignment?"

The jeers and cackles clashed with the buzz, compounding a terrible headache.

Lust jumped in, but Lucifer didn't seem to mind.

"Oh, you know, we just thought—since you've been having so much trouble with her…"

Lust shared a secret smile with Folly. Folly's heart plummeted. Lust's gloating spoke volumes. Payback for pitting her unknowingly against Wisdom. She gritted her teeth. Payback for not telling Lust that Solomon was Wisdom's charge.

"We knew you would jump at the chance to take her out, once and for all."

After a pointed glare, Folly returned her full attention to Lucifer.

"And what makes you think she can be taken out at all?"

Lust opened her mouth, but Lucifer answered.

"She is reeling from the loss of her precious Solomon and the close of her school. Solomon turns more and more to idols and women — which is, in a way—another idol." He smiled at Lust then sought out Religion, bestowing another rare smile on him as well. "She knows war and judgment are coming to the maker's 'chosen people,' and she feels helpless to stop them."

"How did you — ?"

"If there was ever a time to take her out, it is now."

Folly studied the ground before her, blood pounding in her ears. She couldn't face Wisdom again. She couldn't.

"How do you know all of that?" she whispered, finally lifting her eyes to meet his.

"I just do." He looked smug. "You start today. She goes to warn the Israelites of impending judgment. War. Invasion. The usual. You will find her in the city of —"

"But — !"

Her sharp voice burst from her without warning. She bit back the rest, not wanting to see if Lucifer could somehow make her sentence worse.

He glared at her. "It's not a discussion. Go. Distract her. Wreak havoc. It's what you do best."

Folly turned to leave, numb.

"Folly?"

She looked back at him, her face stoic, lifeless.

"Need I remind you what will happen if you fail me?"

She turned and walked out.

It didn't matter if she failed. She was going to her doom, whether she failed or not.

TO BE CONTINUED...

Wisdom & Folly: Sisters, Part Two

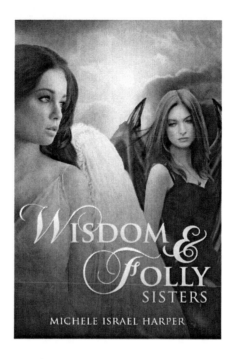

The story doesn't end here!
Discover the conclusion of Wisdom and Folly's tale
in book two.

Will the sisters ever be reconciled?
Or will countless creatures be destroyed in their wake?
Find out in this emotionally-charged battle that spans the ages.

Acknowledgements

First of all, thank YOU for reading my book!

Second, I want to thank all of you who read my chapters as I wrote them and encouraged me. To name a few of the most vocal: Jerry, Amy, Heather, Liv, Sarah, and the members of my writers' group, the Heartland Christian Writers. Joyce, you are such an encouragement, and you and Janet are such wonderful leaders! Thank you Pati, Hannah, Valerie, Nicole, and Tia for your friendship and your amazing tips and advice.

And to my two biggest fans and co-presidents of my fan club, Heather and Beth, you guys are crazy! I love every moment I get to spend with you. Thanks for looking at Every. Single. Version of the cover. (And for making phone companies everywhere regret unlimited texting...)

Sarah Armstrong-Garner. I can't wait until I'm holding *your* book in my hands! Thank you for putting up with all of my "emergency" messages. "What about *this* book cover?" "Does this back cover copy flow well?" "Do you like my website?" You are a saint.

To Sara Helwe: Oh my word, you create an amazing book cover! I am blown away by the way you take my ideas and, *Bam!* Make the most gorgeous cover—so much better than anything I could have thought of. You rock!

My darling Ben. You are the best husband a woman could ask for. Thank you for putting up with my all-nighter writing sprees, and for playing with the kids—where I can't hear them—when I have a deadline. Can you believe I'm actually writing *books* and things? I know. Me either. I love you!

Blaze, Maverick, and Gwenivere. I love so very much watching you grow and learn. You guys are my favorite, and I love every single moment I get to spend with you. I'm so glad God gave you to me! Yes!

I thank my God for each one of you! If I left anyone out, know that you are loved, and I am spacey.

And most importantly, thank You, my King and Savior for giving me these words! This story would never have happened if not for You, my Love. I will praise You for all of my days.

With all my heart, this is for You.

About the Author

Michele Israel Harper is an addict. To books, to writing—if it includes ink and paper, she's all over it. When she found out she could write books instead of simply read them…well, let's just say she's rarely been seen outside of her office since. She adores her writer's group, the Heartland Christian Writers, and has no idea what she would do without the American Christian Fiction Writers. Being voted treasurer for her local Indiana Chapter of ACFW just about sent her into a happy coma. Which, you know, she's very much familiar with since that happens at the end of every good book she reads.

Visit her website at **www.MicheleIsraelHarper.com** if you want to know more about her!

Coming Soon from
Love2ReadLove2Write Publishing

ZOMBIE TAKEOVER

MICHELE ISRAEL HARPER

Candace Marshall hates zombies. As in, loathes, abhors, detests—you get the idea. She also refuses to watch horror movies. You can imagine her complete and utter joy when her boyfriend surprises her with advanced screening tickets to the latest gruesome zombie flick. Annoyance flares into horror as the movie comes to life, and Candace finds herself surrounded by real-life, honest-to-goodness zombies. She learns how to shoot and scream with the best of them and surprises herself with—courage? But, just when Candace thinks it can't get worse than zombies, it does. Don't miss this lighthearted adventure, Book One of the Candace Marshall Chronicles.

Did you like this book?

Authors treasure reviews! (And read them over and over and over…) If you enjoyed this book, would you consider leaving a review on Amazon, Barnes & Noble, Goodreads, or perhaps even your personal blog? Thank you so much!

CPSIA information can be obtained at www.ICGtesting.com
Printed in the USA
LVOW11s0219061115

461373LV00003B/101/P